MS/PE 04
RJ 40

HOMESTAKE LODE

HOMESTAKE LODE

•

G. Sam Carr

AVALON BOOKS
NEW YORK

PRINTED IN THE UNITED STATES OF AMERICA
ON ACID-FREE PAPER
BY HADDON CRAFTSMEN, BLOOMSBURG, PENNSYLVANIA

This story is dedicated to my uncle, Sam Carr, who, while on horseback, was inspecting a water ditch for the Homestake Mining Company when he was shot and killed by a deer hunter.

Prologue

San Francisco, 1878

Lloyd Tevis, President of Wells Fargo; his brother-in-law and business partner, James "Ben" Ali; and Chief of Police for Wells Fargo, J.B. Hume, were gathered in Tevis's office for an emergency meeting to discuss the well-being of their absent partner, George Hearst.

Tevis pulled a folded sheet of paper from his inside coat pocket. He turned to his brother-in-law and said, "Ben, I've just received this letter from George saying that things are going as planned with the Homestake, but he's made some enemies and his life may be in danger."

Tevis shifted his attention to Chief Hume. "Ben and I have done quite well since we teamed up with Hearst. The least we can do is make sure he gets home to his wife and son. I want you to send one of your detectives to the Black Hills. I'll pay his salary and expenses out of my personal account. You just make sure it's the best man you have available."

1

"Yes sir," said Hume. "Will Mr. Hearst be expecting him?"

"No," said Tevis. "Give me his name and I'll write him a letter of introduction."

Chapter One

Dakota Territory, 1878

An awakening sun peeked over the eastern horizon as Wells Fargo Detective Tuck Powells pushed back his Stetson and leaned against the weathered side of the Cheyenne livery stable. He wondered what the commotion was in front of the ticket agent's booth on the far end of the platform as he took out his bag of Bull Durham and papers.

While he built himself a smoke, he thought about Monday morning when Chief Hume had told him he was sending him to the Black Hills to act as a bodyguard for a guy named George Hearst. At first Tuck thought it would help take his mind off Mary Lou. But now he was having second thoughts.

The crowd in front of the agent's office grew large. Tuck wiggled his toes inside his high-heeled boots. It felt good to be on his feet again. The three-day ride from San Francisco on the Union Pacific had been long and boring. The train's seats were well padded, and because the company had bought him a ticket for one of those new Pullman sleeping cars, the conditions weren't half bad. Trouble was, there was nothing to do to pass the time. And, except when he was sacked out, it was impossible to stretch his long legs.

Now as he stared at the Concord stage where nine people would soon be squeezed into an area not much larger than his Pullman berth, he was sure the forty-eight-hour run to Deadwood would seem even longer.

Tuck dug into his shirt pocket and took out a lucifer. He raised his right leg and scraped the match along the rough surface of his Levi's, causing it to burst into flame. He touched the fire to the twisted end of his cigarette and puffed till the tip glowed. Through pursed lips he exhaled a cloud of smoke that blew out the flame.

Just as he flipped the spent match onto the dusty street, he heard someone scream. "Back off, you sons of Satan! And don't try laying a hand on me."

Tuck pictured a female the size of John L. Sullivan. But when the crowd split into two sections he saw a small woman wearing an ankle-length green cape shaking her finger at the ticket agent and saying, "How dare you say I'll have to wait for the next stage! I've got the ticket Mr. Utter sent me and I'm getting on that there buggy." She stomped her foot on the wooden sidewalk and said, "My ticket's as good as those men's. You can just make one of them wait. He'll probably like it, it'll give him a chance to get drunk."

Tuck didn't hear the ticket agent's reply, but he could tell it wasn't to her liking. "I told you, I'm not waiting till tomorrow. I'm goin' today or my name ain't Kelly Ryan!" She turned, picked up her bag, and headed for the stage.

Her no-nonsense strut reminded Tuck of a hen chasing a cat away from her brood of chicks. One thing for sure, she seemed to know what she wanted and would do whatever it took to get it.

She was halfway to the stage when a heavyset man carrying a sample case stepped from the crowd and blocked her way. He shifted his case to his left hand, said something to her, and reached for her bag.

"How dare you?" she yelled as she slapped him so hard the smack echoed across the platform. Tuck ran his hand across his jaw and winced.

The drummer, now protecting his face with his right forearm, turned his back to the young woman.

"How dare you proposition me!" she screamed. "I don't need you and you can bet your life that I won't sit on your lap."

When the red-faced drummer glanced over his shoulder and saw the crowd staring and laughing, he grabbed his bag and waddled up the street.

The woman, her feet spread and hands on hips, stood staring at the drummer till he ducked into a friendly saloon. Then without looking to either side, she picked up her blue-and-red brocaded bag and handed it to the driver. Free of the bag, she stuck her chin in the air, boarded the stage, and took a seat.

While doing so, her hood fell back, giving Tuck a glimpse of a nineteen or twenty-year-old girl with large green eyes, a tiny nose, and long rust-colored hair. Tuck vowed to be mighty careful about anything he said to her. He admired her spunk though. If Mary Lou had been more aggressive, maybe he'd have listened to her.

"Get on board or stay behind," yelled the driver.

Tuck quickly climbed onto the coach, finding that the only empty seat was next to the girl. As he eased himself onto the vacant seat, a crack of the driver's six-horse whip sent the stage lunging forward. Tuck fell back, almost landing in her lap. "Sorry, Miss," he said, bracing himself for a barrage of abuse.

"Don't be silly," she said. "I know it wasn't your fault." Her tone was as calm as a Sunday school teacher's.

Her calmness confused Tuck. Right before his eyes, she'd changed from a cougar to a house cat. Nevertheless, he felt the blood rising to his face and knew he was blushing. Hoping to escape detection, he turned toward the window and pretended to watch the passing landscape.

The constant rattling of harness chains attached to swinging double trees, squeaking leather thorough braces rubbing against the rocking coach, and the repetitious pounding of twenty-four iron-shod hooves on the clay surface of the road had a lulling effect. Tuck closed his eyes and mulled over his meeting with Chief Hume. The chief said the mining tycoon, George Hearst, a business partner of the President of Wells Fargo, had written a letter saying he thought his life was in danger. Because Tuck was available, he was picked to go to the Black Hills and play nursemaid.

Tuck had hoped his next assignment would be a little closer to home, but Wells Fargo had been good to him so he didn't argue when the chief told him where they wanted to send him. In fact he really didn't care where he went as long as he was working again.

When he heard a voice coming from the other side of Kelly, he turned and stared at a sinister one-eyed man wearing a seaman's pea jacket and watch cap. The black patch covering his left eye highlighted the evil cast in his right. The seaman reached out, put his hand on Kelly's knee, and said, "Now you're acting much better. Pretty girls shouldn't go round making a fuss. What you need is a good man to put you in your place. That's me."

Tuck waited for an outburst, but instead, Kelly's jaw tightened and as she shoved his hand away, she said through tight lips, "I don't need any man and if I did, it sure wouldn't be a scroungy animal like you. You better make sure you keep distance between you and me or you won't make it to Deadwood."

The seaman scowled, then drew back his hand and started to swing at Kelly. Before it moved a foot, Tuck reached out and grabbed it. The seaman mumbled something and pulled his hand free, then after giving Tuck a dirty look, he turned his head and gazed out the open window. Kelly acted as though nothing had happened.

Six miners, all wearing crushed-felt hats, leather jackets, flannel shirts, and bib overalls, filled the other two rows of seats. From their conversation, Tuck figured they were hard-rock miners on their way to Lead City. The one the others called John said something about George Hearst, and Tuck's interest perked up. And from the expression on the seaman's face, Tuck wasn't the only one interested.

In a can't-believe-it tone, the one-eyed man asked, "You know George Hearst?"

John paused for a second and said, "Don't really know him, but we worked for him in the Oprah in Nevada and the Ontario in Utah. Now he sent for us to work in the Homestake. He's a good boss; give him a day's work and he'll take care of you."

Tuck took a deep breath; it seemed like everyone, except maybe the girl, had something to do with the same man. Could it be possible that she too knew Hearst? No, that would be too much of a coincidence. Besides, he remembered her saying that a man named Utter had given her a ticket. He wished John would keep talking. Maybe he'd learn more about the man he'd be working for. But John just turned around, reached into his jacket, and pulled out a cribbage board. Then using a coat for a table, the miners cut for partners and started playing.

Six hours and three team changes later, they stopped for supper at a sprawling run-down stage station made of rough logs. Ducking his head to get through the low door, Tuck followed Kelly into the main building. The pungent aroma coming from a pot of simmering meat and vegetables hanging in the large stone fireplace made his mouth water and his gut churn in anticipation. Then when the stationmaster's wife lowered the oven door of a iron cookstove standing in the corner, the fragrance of fresh-baked bread made him want to rush over and help himself.

Instead, he waited for Kelly to take a seat at one end of the long wooden table and he sat at the other. As most of the passengers and crew busied themselves downing huge bowels of venison stew and thick slices of bread, the one-eyed man spent his mealtime drinking whiskey at a bar in the far corner of the room.

As good as it smelled, the meat turned out to be tough and a bit gamy, but Tuck had no trouble getting it down. He had one dish and went back for seconds. It couldn't compare with Mary Lou's cooking, but it was better than his own.

Back on the road with a full stomach, the constant chatter of the card players and the nonstop rocking of the stage made Tuck's eyelids start feeling heavy. He pulled his Stetson down and thought about the peaceful nights he'd spent with Mary Lou in their little apartment in San Francisco. How different she was from Kelly Ryan.

Mary Lou was soft-spoken and always acted like a lady. Not nearly as pretty as Kelly, but she was several years older and obviously better educated. Mary Lou had her own wants and needs, but most of the time she'd sacrifice them for those around her. He couldn't remember her strongly objecting to anything. Not even the dog. She obviously didn't want the dog, but when she saw how he felt about it, she gave in. Too bad, he thought.

Although he was very tired, Tuck was awake most of the long night. But sometime during the wee hours of the morning he must have dozed off. As the stage pulled into Hat Creek Station for breakfast, a change of horses, and a new driver, he discovered Kelly's head resting against his arm.

Less than a minute later she opened her sleep-filled green eyes and looked up at Tuck. Then quick as a frog's tongue she sat up straight and said, "I must've really been tired to do that." After covering her mouth to hide a yawn, she rubbed her eyes and said, "I'm sorry to have bothered you. You can be sure it won't happen again."

Tuck smiled and said, "No problem, Miss."

Without another word, she climbed down from the stage and went into the largest of the sprawling log buildings.

As she walked away, Tuck looked at her with mixed feelings. On one hand he would like to know her better, but on the other hand he wasn't sure of her stability. Kelly Ryan was a real mystery.

But now he was hungry again. He jumped down from the stage and quickly observed the complex of buildings that made up the station. There was not only a telegraph and post office, but also a brewery, bakery, butcher, and blacksmith shop.

When he commented on the size of the place to one of the hostlers, the man said, "That's nothing. We've even got a tunnel that runs from inside the station down to the creek." He pointed to the stream flowing a hundred or so yards behind the buildings, and said, "Several times the Indians tried running us out of here, but with the food we've got on hand, and a way to get fresh water, we can hold them off for months."

Tuck entered the long, and as usual, low-ceilinged room, and heard Kelly say to the new driver, "How much longer is this trip going to take?"

The driver looked at her with a wry smile, lowered his gaze to his tin plate, and said, "The trip's half over, Miss. By this time tomorrow we should be pulling into Deadwood." Tuck watched the driver's smile turn into a grin as he went on to say, "Of course it depends on whether or not the Injuns leave us alone. Or if those dang-blasted stage robbers don't get the idea we're carrying enough gold to make a holdup worthwhile." He went back to eating his fresh sidepork and eggs.

Tuck picked up a plate, went to the big iron cookstove, and filled it with four sunny-side eggs and several strips of uncured bacon. On his way to the table, he noticed the one-eyed man was once again at the bar. Tuck sat down, tore off a chunk of bread, and started sopping up egg yolks. After downing two of the eggs, he poured himself a mug of steaming black coffee from the oversized agate-ware pot standing in the middle of the table.

Tuck finished the rest of his breakfast and thought about the driver's words. He hoped he wasn't serious about the Indians or highwaymen. Not that he would mind a good fight; he'd just rather get to Deadwood without one.

A short time after the stage was rolling again, Kelly turned to Tuck and said, "My name is Kelly Ryan. I don't believe you gave me yours." Her voice was sweet innocence.

Tuck tipped his hat and said, "It's Tuck Powells, Miss Ryan. I'm pleased to make your acquaintance."

With a slight smile and a glow in her eyes, she asked, "Mr. Powells, do you think the driver was telling the truth about the Indians and robbers?"

"Well," he answered, "it seems to me that most of the Indians would have been driven out of the hills by now, and robbers are more apt to stop an outgoing stage rather than this one."

"Why?" she asked as a slight wrinkle formed across her tiny, turned-up nose.

Gosh, she's pretty, he thought. "Outgoing stages are more likely to be carrying gold."

"I sure hope you're right," she said doubtfully.

Since leaving Hat Creek Station, the stage had been climbing steadily. During the first part of the trip they traveled through rolling, sage-covered mounds of red clay. Now they were speeding through thick stands of tall pine and spruce. Scattered along the ridges towering above both sides of the road, outcrops of rimrocks served as platforms for banks of fluffy white clouds. When he spotted a larger-than-usual ledge of gray rocks, Tuck shifted his body to get a better look. Then he felt a tug on his sleeve.

It was Kelly. "I don't ever want to ride on one of these things again. I've never been so uncomfortable in all my life. It seems it's taking us forever to get there and these seats feel like they're made out of iron."

Tuck looked at her and wished he could do something about her comfort. It would be nice to put his arm around her, but she was so young and he was afraid that Mary Lou was watching. Nevertheless he gave her a gentle smile and said, "Not much we can do about it. Try to take your mind off it. Maybe you'll feel better."

"That's not easy to do. Mr. Utter has a job waiting for me and I can't wait to get started. I wish we could go faster."

Her words seemed to make the seaman's head jerk in her direction. His one eye was now bloodshot and his jaw hung slack, loosened by whiskey.

Tuck thought about explaining how, if they went too fast, the dead weight of the coach and passengers quickly sapped the strength of the horses. But instead, he sat staring at the thick dark clouds piling up over the peaks and ridges ahead.

Another tug at his sleeve brought him back to Kelly. "Do you have a gun, Mr. Powells?"

Why would she want to know that? he wondered. "I've got one in my baggage," he said.

She frowned with that wrinkled-up nose again. "But your bag is outside."

"Yes, it's back in the boot with all the others."

Fear showed in her eyes. "That ain't going to help us if we get stopped by Indians or robbers," she said. "But"— she held up her drawstring handbag—"I've got my own pistol. And believe me, I know how to use it."

Funny, Tuck thought. Tough as she was making herself sound, he believed she was trying to convince herself more than anyone else.

Suddenly, as if some heavenly power was testing her, a crack of lightning streaked across the dark sky followed by a deafening clap of thunder and torrents of rain. The card players stopped playing. Kelly slid closer and whispered, "I'm trying to get away from that nasty man."

Tuck nodded and lowered the leather curtains on his side of the stage. On the opposite side, the miner, John, did the same.

The curtains helped, but every time a fierce streak of lightning crashed to earth, Tuck felt Kelly shiver. It was as if God had chosen them to witness his demonstration of power. Rain hit the stage with such force it felt as if they were traveling beneath a giant waterfall. Tuck hoped the driver could follow the road. "How long is this bloody storm going to last?" one of the miners asked.

No one answered.

The storm had placed Tuck in a quandary. Kelly's obvious attempt for protection had her pressed so tight against him that a cigarette paper wouldn't fit between them. He hadn't been with a woman since Mary Lou and the feel of Kelly and the smell of her perfume was causing the expected results. He knew he should ask her to move, but he didn't want to. Fact was, he liked the feel of her next to him. It made him realize how much he missed a woman's warm touch. He was tempted to let down his guard and put his arm around her. He even thought he read in her eyes that it was what she wanted too. But he couldn't risk a rejection, so he leaned back and folded his arms across his chest.

When the storm finally passed, the driver's whip sent a report like firecrackers crashing through the rain-washed air. The stage picked up speed to make up for some of the time they lost.

Several hours later, when they topped a long steep grade, the driver pulled up and leaned over the side. "If you folks want to stretch your legs, now's the time," he yelled.

When Tuck stepped down from the stage, the driver came up to him and pulled him aside. "How about you riding up top with us? We're going to need some help getting down into the canyon."

This was totally unexpected. "How can I help?" Tuck asked.

The driver puckered up and spit a mouthful of tobacco juice. After using his sleeve to wipe his lips, he said, "If the horses get the notion the stage is going to overtake them, they try to go faster. Next thing we know we're liable to be rolling head over heels down the mountain." He paused. "I don't think you folks would like that and I know me and the horses won't."

Tuck thought for a second, then said, "I guess some fresh air wouldn't hurt and I used to work my father's team, but it looks to me like driving farm horses is a lot different than holding back a span of runaways. Maybe you should have someone with more experience."

"I expect you'll do just fine," the driver said as he patted Tuck on the back. "I'll take care of the horses. I'll need you to keep a steady strain on the brake. And with the messenger handling the line, we'll make it."

Tuck wasn't sure what the messenger would be doing but he didn't want to sound stupid so he walked to the edge of the canyon and peered down to its floor. His heart dropped to his stomach; the job looked impossible. A steep narrow road had been carved out of the canyon wall. He turned to the driver and asked, "You mean this is the only road into Deadwood?"

"No, but it's the best one. Let's get on with it."

After the passengers boarded, Tuck took a seat alongside the driver. The messenger climbed on top of the stage, picked up a coil of heavy rope, and tied one end to the baggage rail.

The driver eased the stage over the edge and they started the zigzag trip to the bottom. On the right was an almost vertical tree-covered mountain. On the left, a sheer drop to the canyon floor. Tuck felt the hair rising on the back of his neck. Every time they rolled over a stone or hit a rut, the heavy stage creaked and groaned as it jerked to one side or the other.

Tuck held his foot tight against the brake handle. The driver talked constantly to the horses. "Easy now. That's the way. Whoa. Pull back. Giddy up now." With each set of words he pulled up or let out on the reins.

Tuck finally got the feel of things and relaxed a bit. Then all of a sudden, the rear wheels slid toward the edge, leaving nothing but air between them and the canyon floor. Tuck was sure it was going to topple. The driver pulled on the reins and yelled, "Get a hold on something!"

The messenger leaped from the stage and scrambled to a nearby pine tree. He quickly took a turn around the tree and held fast. The rope stretched as tight as a fiddle string, but the stage remained upright.

Tuck took a deep breath and looked at the driver. "Whew! That was close. I was ready to jump."

"Good thing you didn't. We'd be goners for sure."

The driver leaned over, stared down at the left rear wheel, and said, "The durn wheel is off the edge. We've got to be mighty careful." He turned to Tuck. "Yell inside and tell everyone to move to the right. That'll help shift the weight."

After doing as he was told, Tuck took another look at the driver. He was amazed at how calm the driver remained as every couple of seconds he leaned over the side and checked the wheel. When satisfied all four wheels were on solid ground, he told the messenger to slack off and get back on board. Then, as if nothing had happened, they resumed their journey down the mountain.

It seemed like a lifetime later that the road leveled out and they came upon another group of log buildings. A sign on the largest one read *TEN-MILE RANCH*. They'd reached the last stop before Deadwood.

Soon as the driver pulled up, two hostlers ran forward and unhooked the team. While they were doing that, two others led out six alabaster-white horses. They were the best-matched team Tuck had ever seen. When the driver saw him admiring them, he said, "These are our show horses. We only use them to take the stage in and out of Deadwood. They know the route as good or better than most of the drivers."

Tuck moved alongside the left lead horse and ran his fingers through its long white mane. The driver did the same to the one on the right. "How would you like to ride the box all the way into Deadwood?"

Tuck smiled and asked, "I won't have to work the brake, will I?"

The driver pursed his lips and let go a cheek full of tobacco juice. "Not this time. You can lean back and enjoy the fresh air and watch these horses strut their stuff."

Tuck said okay and started toward the station where he saw Kelly waiting.

"Mind if I join you for breakfast, Mr. Powells?"

"Not at all, Miss Kelly." He thought about the hours she'd been against him and how she'd rekindled longings that he was trying to forget.

"When you told us to move to the right of the stage, I thought I'd die." She paused, and said, "I was sure that dirty seaman would have his hands all over me."

"Did he?" Tuck asked.

"No. He was holding on to the window so tight he didn't try anything."

"That's good," says Tuck.

"Not that good. I still had to put up with his stench. It almost made me sick." She turned loose his arm and they went inside.

While Tuck was eating his usual breakfast of meat and eggs, Kelly limited herself to small chunks of bread that she tore from a slice and gently placed in her mouth. Tuck wondered if her loss of appetite was because he'd told her he was going to stay up in the driver's box. Could it be because she was worried about the one-eyed man making a pass at her? He decided to make sure the seaman behaved himself.

Kelly got up and excused herself. As soon as she was

out the door, Tuck moved slowly to the bar and pointed his finger at the one-eyed man. "Mister, I don't know what your name is—nor do I want to know. But I'll tell you this: make one more move on that girl and you'll answer to me. You get the message?"

The one-eyed man scowled, downed his shot of whiskey, and said, "Who wants her anyway? Stuck-up little wench. There'll be plenty of time to get her after we get to Deadwood. That is if I want her." He poured himself another shot. Tuck hoped it was just the whiskey talking.

Tuck went outside and saw Kelly, and they walked back to the stage together. He helped her inside and then climbed into the box and squeezed between the driver and messenger. A crack of the whip over the backs of the triple span of horses, and they were on their way.

For the first time Tuck was able to relax and enjoy the sights. The road ran alongside a fast-flowing stream that bounced and bubbled its way through clumps of white birch trees, olive-colored aspens, and dark green chokecherry bushes heavily loaded with black ripe fruit. Raspberry plants clung to the sides of the canyon. Robins, magpies, bluebirds, and others he couldn't identify fluttered in and out of the fruit-filled branches. In almost any direction he looked, he spotted a squirrel, rabbit, groundhog, or deer. He had to admit that as wild and uncivilized as the surroundings appeared, they were stunning.

The driver jerked his head to his left and said, "We're going to follow this creek all the way into Deadwood." He paused to spit over the side. "Up the road a piece, this creek joins up with one running down Gold Run Gulch. If Fred Doten is waiting with his hack at the junction, I'll stop so anyone going to Lead City can get off and ride with him. Fred will get them to Lead City about the same time we'll be pulling into Deadwood."

Tuck wondered if Kelly would be getting off. He remembered her saying she had a job waiting in Lead City. What kind of a job? he wondered. But that wasn't his business. He had his own job to do and even though it too was in Lead City, he decided to go on to Deadwood with the stage. But then he thought of the one-eyed seaman and had a funny feeling that Kelly hadn't heard the last of him. What's more, as tough as she tried to make herself sound, Tuck knew she'd be no match for the drunken bum.

He was still thinking about Kelly when the stage rounded a sharp bend and Tuck spotted them. About three hundred yards ahead, two masked men stood in the middle of the road with pistols pointed at the stage. One of them fired into the air. The driver cracked his whip. The messenger pumped his shotgun. Tuck reached for his .45 only to remember it was still in his bag. There was nothing he could do but hope for the best.

"Out of my way, you slimy lizards," bellowed the driver.

Smoke belched from the outlaws' pistols. The driver stood up, dropped the reins, and fell forward out of the box. Tuck looked over the front and spotted the driver's arms and shoulders hanging over the tongue. His dragging feet sent dust flying behind them. Tuck started down to help him, but soon as he got one leg over the front, the driver's body broke loose and disappeared beneath the stage.

When the messenger let go with both barrels of his shotgun, the blast caused Tuck's ears to ring and the smell of gunpowder burned his nostrils. He didn't know if the shots hit one of the robbers or not, but before the smoke cleared, the messenger dropped his shotgun and fell forward. Tuck grabbed the messenger's boot. But as he tried to get a firmer grip, the boot came off and the wounded messenger dropped to the ground. Tuck felt both right wheels rise and drop as they crossed the man's body.

Tuck flung the empty boot aside and grabbed the reins. The horses were now running at full speed toward the outlaws. They lowered their pistols and leaped aside. Tuck looked at the handful of leather and wondered which rein controlled which horse. He'd never handled six horses before and figured if he pulled back on the wrong one, it would throw the horses out of cadence and cause the stage to roll over.

He bunched the most-worn sections of the heavy leather straps in his hands and pulled back on all of them at the same time. The horses kept running. When they sped past the junction, he yelled to the waiting hack man, "They tried to hold us up!" He pulled back on the reins again. As before, none of the horses responded. Tuck hoped the driver was right when he said they knew where they were going.

From the backs of the speeding horses, globs of white frothy sweat sprayed Tuck's face, arms, and chest. Some of it mixed with his own sweat, slid down his cheeks, and into his mouth; it tasted like a chunk of rock salt. He tried spitting but his mouth was too dry. Surely it was just a matter of time before the stage tipped over.

Suddenly they rounded another bend and entered the town. The horses maintained their frightening speed. Tuck jerked the reins again. It didn't even slow them down. But then a strange thing happened. When they got to the stage platform in front of the post office, the gasping, sweat-drenched horses pulled up and stopped in their tracks.

Chapter Two

Kelly hoped her smile hid the disappointment she felt when Tuck told her he was going to finish the trip in the driver's box.

When Tuck helped her on board, she took his seat next to the window, making sure there was plenty of space between her and the one-eyed man. In spite of having to share her seat with this disgusting man, she wanted to believe it was safer having Tuck up there helping the driver. But in her heart she knew she'd much rather have him here next to her. Maybe he'd even put his arm around her. Oh, well, there was nothing she could do about it now. Best thing was to sit back and hope the trip didn't take much longer and that she'd find some way to make Tuck take a greater interest in her.

Kelly glanced at the other passengers. They were all men that looked dirty and probably smelled as bad as they looked. Especially the one-eyed man who kept staring at her with that bloodshot eye. It made her feel naked. At least the others were so wrapped up in their card game they weren't paying her much notice. She wondered if the one-eyed man started bothering her, would any of them come to her aid? She wasn't afraid of any of them, but with no place to run, she had to depend on her little pistol to keep her safe. She'd never had to shoot it and wasn't too sure she remembered how.

Funny how Tuck Powells was so different. It wasn't only his wavy blond hair, deep blue eyes, and handsome face. He looked like a man who could be trusted. That trust didn't come easily to Kelly. She really had no use for men, especially her father. He was a no-good bum. If it hadn't been for her mother, they'd have starved. Up to now she thought all men were the same. They took everything a woman could give, used her for a while, and then moved on. She had wised up early and refused to fall into their trap.

On the other hand, Tuck was different. She'd only met him a couple of days ago and didn't know much about him, but she had this wonderful feeling that he was something special. She liked the fact he could look at her without making her feel uncomfortable. And when she fell asleep and rested her head on his arm, he didn't try to read anything into it. Remembering it brought back the fact that she thought she'd die of embarrassment when she woke up and realized what she had been doing. Just to make sure he didn't get the wrong idea, she had to let him know it was an accident. Actually the whole thing seemed to embarrass him as much as it did her. Without a doubt, Tuck Powells was an unusual man.

After Tuck had agreed to help out in the box, it didn't take long for the one-eyed man to start in. At first it was the glaring way he looked at her. A look that make goose bumps cover her skin. Then when he mumbled something she couldn't make out, she turned and stared out the window. He slid closer and said, "You don't have to be afraid of me. I've got high-level friends in Lead City and if you're nice to me, I'll introduce you to them." He sounded just like she imagined Simon Legree would have sounded to Little Nell.

She reached in her bag and took her pistol in hand as she looked him in the eye and said, "I don't need you or your friends. Now leave me alone or I'm going to start yelling for the driver to stop the stage."

Then all of a sudden the stage jerked to the left, rocked to one side, and felt like it was going to tip over. She let go of her pistol, crossed herself, and held her breath. She glanced at the others. They looked as scared as she felt. The card players appeared to be suspended in time. No one moved.

She reached for the door, ready to jump. But when she looked out and saw nothing but the canyon floor below, she changed her mind. Then she heard Tuck telling everyone to shift to the right. Scared as she was, she grinned to see the seaman, now not so tough, grasping the window ledge with both hands. He didn't even notice when she slid next to him.

Soon as they started moving again, she quickly moved back to her side of the coach. By the time she'd crossed herself several more times they'd leveled off and picked up speed. The seaman was no longer a threat. For the rest of the trip to Ten-Mile Ranch, he didn't say another word.

At breakfast when she mentioned to Tuck how the seaman had acted, he said not to worry about it and to ignore him, but she didn't have to. After leaving Ten-Mile Ranch the seaman stayed glued to his side. He didn't even try to talk to her. But she still felt uncomfortable when she caught him looking at her out of the corner of his eye. Thank goodness he didn't go any further.

The tranquil sounds of iron-rimmed wheels turning on hard ground, wood and leather rubbing together, and the clopping of the horses' hooves were suddenly interrupted by gunshots. Kelly sat up straight. She heard yelling.

The stage surged forward with a jolt. Kelly was thrown back against her seat. What was happening? It had to be bad. She caught a glimpse of someone falling, but couldn't tell who it was. Sweat ran down her back. She thought she heard Tuck's voice and felt better. But maybe it wasn't him. There was so much confusion she couldn't be sure.

Kelly's hands ached from trying to hold on. She knew they were going too fast and if the stage tipped over they'd all be killed.

Suddenly the passing scenery changed from trees and rocks to buildings. They'd entered Deadwood. Thank heavens! Maybe soon she could get out and make sure Tuck was safe.

When the stage finally stopped, Kelly gathered her skirts and climbed down. Her gaze shot up to the driver's box. Empty! She looked around. Neither Tuck, the driver, nor the messenger were anywhere to be seen.

Within a minute, townspeople came running from all directions, all trying to talk at the same time. Kelly wanted to ask if anyone had seen Mr. Powells, but was afraid of what she might hear. She didn't want to believe that he'd been killed along with the driver and messenger.

A tall, slender, middle-aged man came over. He had a large black, droopy mustache, and wore a broad-brimmed hat. A badge was pinned to his black leather vest.

"Let's have a little quiet here. I can't hear myself think." The lawman turned to John and started questioning the miners.

Kelly gritted her teeth. Why was he wasting time? None of them knew what happened. He should go back and see if Tuck or any of the stage crew was still alive.

The lawman was talking to the one-eyed seaman when a strange-looking wagon driven by a wiry, gray-haired man pulled to a stop behind the stage. He stood up in his wagon and yelled out, "The stage driver was killed. The messenger is hurt, but still alive."

The man's eyes swept over the crowd. "Say, where's that young fella that had the reins when the stage went through Pluma?"

Kelly took a deep breath and moved closer. Maybe he was talking about Mr. Powells. Maybe he survived the shooting. But where could he be? Maybe he was wounded and fell off. What if he was lying somewhere along the road?

She looked up at the lawman. "My name is Kelly Ryan and I was a passenger on the stage. Are you the sheriff?"

"Yes, ma'am. Can you tell me what went on?"

Kelly shook her head and said, "No, sir. I was inside but something must have happened to Mr. Powells. He was up in the box." She pointed to the wagon driver. "That man over there said he saw him on the stage after the shooting was over. But he has disappeared. I just know he was wounded and fell off. Why ain't you going back to look for him?"

Concern showed in the sheriff's pale-blue eyes as he said, "We'll do what has to be done, Miss."

She followed as he walked over to the driver of the hack and said, "Howdy, Fred. I understand you was waiting at Pluma for the stage." He gestured to Kelly. "This young lady says you saw a stranger handling the reins when it went through?"

"Sure did, Seth. The Homestake people hired me to pick up a contract crew of Cousin Jacks." He rubbed his chin. "Like you say, I was waiting there figuring it would be along any minute. Then I heard the shots."

"Did you see who was shooting?"

"Nope. Just the stage rounding the bend. It was going as fast as them horses could go. Reminded me of a cat with a tomato can tied to his tail. A stranger was in the driver's box. He was wearing a sheepskin coat and yelling at the top of his lungs."

"And that's the last time you saw the stranger?"

"Yep."

Sheriff Bullock doffed his hat and scratched his head. "That's curious. These folks say the box was empty as a miner's pocket afore payday when the stage came to a stop. You going back to Lead City now?"

"Yep. I'll take off soon as you give me the word and I can round up my passengers." The driver faced the crowd. "Any of you folks headed for Lead City can climb on my back. We'll pull out in a couple of minutes."

The one-eyed man asked the driver for directions to the livery stable. Kelly was glad. At least he'd be out of her life. She reached down and picked up her brocaded garment bag. The hack man offered to take her bag from her and said, "Here, Miss. Let me have that. My name's Fred Doten."

Kelly said, "Thanks, but I can handle my own bag."

He shrugged, smiled, and said, "Suit yourself, but I think maybe you should ride up front with me. Cousin Jacks have a lot of superstitions and one of them is that redheaded women are bad luck. Wouldn't be surprised if they think you caused the problems on the stage."

"Cousin Jacks?" Kelly asked.

He grinned and said, "That's what we call Cornish miners."

Kelly wondered why, but didn't want to take the time to find out. She smiled at Doten and said, "Thank you for the advice, but if one of them starts anything, the undertaker is going to have another customer before this day is over." She knew she was being rude, but, except for Tuck, most men who said they only wanted to help really wanted something else.

The hack driver gave her a funny look as he said, "Have it your own way, ma'am, but don't say I didn't warn you."

Then Kelly noticed a bag still on the platform. It must be Tuck's. Should she take care of it for him? She'd like too, but she had all she could do to take care of her own. Why, she wondered, hadn't the sheriff sent someone out to try to find Tuck? "Better get aboard, Miss," said the driver.

She handed her bag up to him and discovered the only vacant seat was next to him. "I guess you're going to ride up here with me whether you like it or not," he said with a wry grin. "But don't worry, I won't bite. Just put your foot on the hub and give me your hand."

Kelly climbed up and sat next to him.

Just as they were ready to get under way, Sheriff Bullock pulled his bigheaded gray horse alongside the wagon. "Fred, I'd appreciate it if you went back the way you came in and keep an eye out for the young fella that seems to have disappeared. I'm going to round up some men and see if we can pick up the trail of the killers."

Kelly felt better. Being up front would make it easier to look for Tuck.

When one of the miners said something about redheaded women, she ignored him. She didn't have time for anything except finding the only man who really had befriended her.

Soon as they left Deadwood, the driver took his time and whenever he spotted a place where a body could be hidden, he stopped and climbed down to take a look. Each time Kelly held her breath and prayed that Tuck was still alive.

They'd stopped at a half dozen places when they came to a fork in the road. "This is Pluma, where I was waiting." Fred Doten pointed to the left fork and said, "The stage came down that road. The stranger was on board when it passed." He snapped the reins over the rumps of the team and said, "Giddy up." The horses started running up the right fork. "This is Gold Run Creek. We'll follow it into Lead City."

Kelly sighed. She prayed their failure to locate Tuck didn't mean something bad had happened to him. But there was nothing more she could do now. She turned to the driver and asked, "Mr. Doten, do you know Mr. Charley Utter?"

Her words caused the driver to snap his head in her direction. "Don't tell me you're one of his girls?"

"I'm going to be one of his actresses," Kelly said. "And I'll bet in no time I'll be the star of the show." Kelly crossed her arms. "I want to prove to Mr. Utter that he didn't waste his money when he paid my way out here. I know I'm a good actress. In a few weeks, everybody'll be saying the same thing."

"Actress?" asked Fred Doten.

"Yes. I answered an advertisement in the San Francisco newspaper." She was confused. Why was he shaking his head? "The man I talked to said it was a once-in-a-lifetime opportunity."

Almost under his breath, Doten said, "If you only knew."

"What do you mean by that?" Kelly asked.

A heavy frown formed on the driver's face. "Miss. Charley Utter has a bad reputation. I don't suppose I could talk you out of taking that job?"

Kelly studied his expression. Was he setting her up? She thought about her empty purse. What could she do now? She didn't have any money left or any other place to go. She tried to smile as she said, "Of course not; this is my big chance."

Fred Doten shook his head again. "Before you go too far, I think you should know a lot more about Charley Utter's place."

She was getting weary of this conversation. "I know all I need to know." She pulled her cape tighter around her and turned away.

A few minutes later they entered the outskirts of a small city where most of the buildings looked new or were still under construction. She figured they were near the center of town when they turned right on Mill Street. Halfway up the block, the driver pulled back on the reins. "Whoa there." The hack stopped in front of a square-fronted two-story wood building. A large block-lettered sign read:

DANCE PALACE
Charley Utter—Proprietor

"Here ya are, Miss Kelly. I sure hope you know what you're doing."

"Thanks for your concern, but I can take care of myself." She stepped down onto the wooden sidewalk and took her bag from the driver's outstretched hand. Then she turned, pushed open a pair of bat-wing doors, and went inside.

When her eyes adjusted to the dim light, she found herself in a large smoke-filled room crowded with people, mostly men, dressed in all types of attire. One man wore a top hat and tails, several were dressed as cowboys, some in business suits, but the majority wore bib overalls and flannel shirts. The dozen or so women wore skimpy red-and-white costumes over black fishnet stockings.

Kelly wasn't sure what kind of place she was in. When she faced one direction she thought she was in one of her father's old hangouts. But when she turned around, it was like being in a theater. Across the end wall of the saloon side stood an ornate mahogany bar over which hung a life-sized painting of a reclining woman wearing even less than the bar girls. Beneath the painting, a wall-to-wall mirror made the room appear even larger than it actually was.

On the theater side was a stage that looked to be ten or twelve feet deep. But unlike the bar, it did not run the full length of the wall. The backdrop was a mural of dancing ladies wearing long shimmering pink gowns. Velvet drapes provided the finishing touch. To the left of the stage, a curved stairway led to a balcony circling the entire room.

Crowded between the bar and stage were dozens of round wooden tables surrounded by armchairs. Kelly pondered the layout and decided that when the show started, they probably closed the bar. It wasn't good but she could live with that.

Over her shoulder she spotted the heavyset, slick-haired bartender coming toward her. When they were face to face, he gave his waxed handlebar moustache a twist and asked, "Something I can do for you, lady?"

"Why yes," she said. "You can tell Mr. Utter that the actress, Miss Kelly Ryan, has arrived and would like to make his acquaintance."

The bartender smirked. "You're Kelly Ryan?"

This wasn't going right. She wanted to say, "*Miss* Kelly Ryan to you," but thought better of it. Instead she smiled and said, "Yes, I am Kelly Ryan."

The bartender stared at her for a second, gave her a wink, rubbed his hands on his apron, and patted her on the head. "Miss Kelly Ryan. Actress, you say." He was still laughing when he went to the end of the bar, pushed aside a red-velvet drape, and disappeared from sight.

Kelly clinched her fists and was ready to explode. Instead, she took a deep breath and hoped Charley Utter wasn't as unpleasant as the bartender. She looked around and noticed that she had become the center of attention. Too bad. She didn't care. These were not the kind of people she wanted to impress. She looked up at the balcony and wondered if her dressing room was behind one of the many doors.

Out of the corner of her eye Kelly watched men pawing at the women. What made her sicker was the fact that the women laughed and seemed to enjoy the attention. The whole scene was disgusting. How could those women allow those dirty creatures to touch them? What pigs!

Then the drape opened, and the bartender stepped out and held it back for a slightly built man dressed in trousers and vest of black broadcloth beneath a Prince Albert coat. Across his belly hung a watch chain of gold coins. His hair fell to his shoulders and he sported a longhorn mustache. He had the look and smell of a man who had recently bathed.

He smiled and offered his hand to Kelly. "Well, well, so you are my new girl from San Francisco. I trust you had a pleasant trip and are ready to go to work."

"Mr. Utter?" said Kelly.

"That's right, Colorado Charley Utter. I own this place. The bartender tells me your name is Kelly Ryan." He leaned back and ran his gaze from her shoes to her head.

"Not bad. Looks like the San Francisco agency earned their money this time."

Kelly frowned. "Mr. Utter, that man at the agency said I was hired as an actress. If that's not the case, I believe we had better discuss the matter immediately."

Utter's face broke into a wide grin. "Actress! I said I wanted entertainers. You entertain my customers by giving them whatever they're willing to pay for. Then twice a night, you dance in the cancan line."

He motioned to a tall, buxom blond wearing next to nothing and said, "Trixie, come here. This is Kelly, show her to her room and give her an outfit. The sooner she gets started, the sooner I'll get my money back."

But Kelly had heard enough. "Mr. Utter, I'm not going to be one of your girls. I happen to be a serious actress. Unless you have a legitimate part in a legitimate play, I'm afraid I must seek employment elsewhere." She reached down, picked up her bag, and started for the door.

Charley Utter grabbed the hood of her cape. "You're not going anywhere till I get the three hundred dollars I've invested in you. Now, you follow Trixie or I'll drag you right up the stairs. And when I get done with you, you won't be quite so uppity."

The look in his eyes stopped her from saying anything else. As much as she hated to, for now she'd have to play his game and wait for a chance to escape.

Trixie took Kelly's hand and smiled. As they walked away, Trixie said, "It's not too bad. We'll go to your room and talk. Charley can be awfully mean when he's mad."

Well, she thought, she'd soon show Mr. Charley Utter that she wasn't like the other women. And the way she felt now, it wouldn't be long.

At the top of the stairs, Kelly followed Trixie into a tiny box of a room. A single bed pushed against one wall was the main piece of furniture. Keeping the bed company was a wooden box supporting a smoke-stained kerosene lamp. On the opposite wall was a washstand beneath an unframed mirror. A scuffed table accompanied by two chairs sat beneath an uncurtained window. On the wall nearest the foot of the bed was a three-foot-long shelf with a floor-length, white muslin curtain nailed to its edges.

As soon as the door closed, Kelly flung her bag on the bed, opened her drawstring bag, and pulled out the derringer. "That son of Satan is not going to treat me like that. I'm going down there right now and I'll show him who he's dealing with." Kelly started for the door.

Trixie quickly blocked Kelly's path, grabbed her by her shoulders, and pushed her onto the bed. "Are you crazy, girl? You haven't got a chance against that man. Unless you've got the three hundred dollars, you're going to have to stay and work until you can pay him off."

Through burning eyes, Kelly looked up at Trixie. "But I'm an actress. I can't do the things you girls do. Even if I could, I wouldn't."

Trixie shook her head as she said, "Honey, you might as well get it through your brain that you're here to separate those men from their gold. It don't matter to Charley whether you like it or not. It's your job and you've got to make the best of it. If you don't, he'll make sure you wish you had."

Kelly looked defeated as she asked, "What will he do?"

Trixie wrapped her arms around Kelly and said, "He's a mean man. He'll do whatever it takes to break you. It don't make a bit of difference to him if you live or die, long as you live long enough to get him back his investment in you."

Kelly fought to hold back the tears, but couldn't. Large drops welled up from the corners of her eyes and rolled down her cheeks as she said, "Trixie, please help me get away from here."

Trixie took the towel from the washstand and handed it to Kelly. "Calm down now," she said. "You've got to pull yourself together. I'll go down and tell Charley you're sick from the stagecoach trip and can't accommodate any customers for a couple of days. But you'll still have to hustle drinks."

While the words were sinking in, Trixie went to the foot of the bed and pulled aside the curtain covering the garments hanging on a wooden pole. She took down a red girdle, a flared bustle, a white V-necked bodice, black fishnet stockings, and long black fingerless gloves and dropped them on the bed. "You get dressed, then come downstairs. I'll show you the ropes."

At the door, Trixie turned and said, "You say you're an actress. Well, honey, you'll never get a more important role than you've got right now. Make it look good and you just might get out of this." She then hurried out the door, closing it behind her.

While staring at the closed door, Kelly thought about her father and how much the drunken men downstairs reminded her of him. He'd been cruel to her mother, to Kelly, and all the children—even to the dog. Too bad Charley Utter couldn't meet the same fate her father did. She pictured that rainy day he was staggering home from a saloon and fell beneath the wheels of a trolley. She didn't shed a tear for him that day, or any day since.

Kelly still wondered why her mother missed him. It seemed she had to have a man to take care of. It was even worse after her father was killed. He was only dead a few weeks when her mother took up with another man. He stayed a while and then moved on. No sooner had he left than she brought home another.

Now, just thinking about it was making her sick. To think she once again had to put up with drunken, evil men—she wasn't sure she could do it.

Kelly stared into the mirror and saw a stranger staring back. She was a mess. Her eyes were puffy and the color of hot coals. She poured water from a ceramic pitcher into a matching washbowl, then she dipped the end of the towel into the cool water and pressed it against her eyes.

Soon as the redness faded, she put on the skimpy outfit.

She felt mortified. How could she go downstairs? She was about to take it off and put on her own clothes when she remembered Trixie's warning. She prayed she'd have the strength to endure whatever was about to happen.

After straightening the seams in the long stockings, she took a brush from her bag and brushed her hair till the long, silky, rust-colored strands shined. She put on powder and rouge and added a bit of color to her lips. Even if she didn't like what she was doing, she was going to look good doing it.

On her way to the door, she stopped, went back to the bed, picked up her little pistol, and stuck it inside her bodice. The feel of it there gave her a sense of safety.

'As Kelly held tight to the handrail and walked slowly down the stairs, she hoped no one noticed her knees shaking. She searched the crowd for Trixie. When she spotted her by the bar, Kelly headed in her direction.

She'd only taken a few steps when a drunken, unshaven man in miner's garb blocked her path and said, "Hi there, sweetie. What say you and I get better acquainted?"

Kelly pushed him aside and continued toward Trixie, "Uppity tramp!" she heard him say.

The tables were so close together that, try as she did, it was impossible not to brush up against the men seated near her path. To a man they tried to touch her wherever they could. Each time one of them made contact, she felt the blood rush to her face. How was she going to put up with this without losing her temper?

When Trixie saw her, she took Kelly's arm and led her to a less-crowded spot near one end of the bar and said, "Don't let these hound dogs bother you. Most of them are just lonesome."

Kelly squeezed Trixie's arm and said, "I'll never feel right doing this. I'm not sure I'm going to be able to go through with it. I've got to find a way out of here."

"Don't start that again!" whispered Trixie. "You've got

to make the best of it. Grab a tray and follow me—I'll show you how to take drink orders."

Kelly watched as Trixie stepped briskly up to a table of men clamoring for service. "What'll you have, boys?" As she wrote down their order, one of the men reached up and grabbed her. Trixie playfully knocked his hand away and said, "You have to pay for that, buster. Nothing free here."

Chills ran down Kelly's back. No way she'd be able to let one of them to do that to her and get off so easy.

For the next half-hour Kelly tagged along while Trixie made several trips to the bar. Finally, the bartender said, "It's about time you're on your own. Go work the tables by the stage."

Kelly felt her heart drop. She held tight to her tray and headed toward the stage.

"Hey, carrot top. Come over and take our order." She turned and saw it was a fat man with food stains covering his checkered vest. He was seated at a table with three other equally unkempt individuals.

Kelly put on a no-nonsense expression and said, "What can I get you gentlemen?"

The fat man said, "Bring us a bottle and four glasses. No, make it five. One for you." When he smiled, she noticed his urgent need of a dentist.

Kelly gave him a wry smile, and said, "I don't drink. But thank you anyway." She went to the bar, picked up and delivered their order, took their money, and then moved to another table.

For four straight hours, with only minor incidents and without losing her temper, Kelly worked her end of the room. As time passed, she felt better and began to think she might be able to survive for a few days. Then the bartender said, "Mr. Utter wants to see you."

Her blood turned to ice. She stared at him and said, "I'm doing my job. What does he want with me?"

"How would I know, girl? I don't question the boss and you'd better not either. Just get yourself behind that curtain.

He's in his office and if I was you, I wouldn't make him come out looking for you. He don't like to wait."

Before she had a chance to move, the drape was pushed aside and Charley Utter, sporting a big smile, stepped out saying, "Well, my little actress, you've proved you can wait tables. Now, we'll see if you can really earn your money."

She felt sweat forming on her brow. "Didn't Trixie tell you I'm feeling sick from the stagecoach ride?"

"Girl, this guy's so drunk he won't even notice. He's got a roll of greenbacks big enough to choke a horse and we're going to get it from him."

Kelly clenched her fists and stepped back. "You'll have to get someone else. I'm not going to do it."

Utter's face turned scarlet. He grabbed her by the arm, dragged her behind the drape, and flung her against the wall, sending pain pulsing through her.

"Listen, woman, you've got to learn! Don't you ever tell me you're not going to do something. The man in my office wants you bad, and he willing to pay for it. You're going in there and make him happy."

When Kelly opened her mouth to scream, he hit her, knocking her to the floor. Then he reached down and jerked her to her feet by her hair. She felt helpless, a little girl again and afraid to fight. "I'm going to give you one more chance," said Utter. "You go in there and give that man his money's worth." He opened the door and flung her inside.

Flying into the room, she came face to face with the one-eyed seaman. He looked even worse than he did on the stage. His eye was blood red, and slimy drops of spittle clung to the corners of his mouth.

"Surprised to see me, Miss Kelly Ryan? You ain't got no cowboy now. I told you if you was nice to me I'd take care of you. Now it's too late."

He reached out to grab her. Kelly dodged. He lunged and she stepped aside and said, "Leave me alone or I'll scream."

He laughed and said, "Go ahead and scream. I've paid Utter for you and I'm going to get what I paid for." He spread his arms and came at her.

She tried to duck under his right arm, but he was too fast. He grabbed the neck of her bodice, ripping it. He let go and caught hold of her hair, pulling her to him. She tried to break free, but his grip jerked her head back. But now she was mad. Kicking and punching, she yelled, "Leave me alone, I said! Touch me and I'll kill you!"

She was wasting her breath. He hit her with a clenched fist, sending her flying across the room. She landed on her back on top of the table Charley Utter used for a desk. Groggy from the blow, she couldn't move. He stumbled to her and grabbed her legs. She kicked but he was too strong.

Kelly was terrified now. There was no telling how far this depraved animal would go to force himself on her. Bleeding and broken, she feared for her life. She reached between her breasts and felt the warm metal of her little derringer. She pulled it out, pointed, and fired.

The sound reverberated through Charley Utter's office. The one-eyed seaman had a small blood-oozing hole above his eyepatch. Then he fell forward on top of her.

Kelly held back the urge to scream as she quickly rolled him off her. He dropped to the floor and didn't move. She stood up and looked around. Someone must have heard the shot. Any minute, one of them could come bursting into the room.

Kelly put her ear to the door. Didn't sound like anyone was coming. Maybe they didn't hear the shot. She looked around and spotted another door on the opposite wall. She rushed to it, turned the knob, opened it a sliver, and peeked out onto a back alley.

There was no one in sight. She trembled. A cold chill went through her. She covered herself with the remnants of her torn blouse, bolted down the back steps, and ran into the dark alley.

Chapter Three

Soon as the horses stopped, Tuck jumped from the stage and ducked behind the post office. This was no time to answer a bunch of questions and maybe wind up in the newspaper. His hands shook. Cramps knotted his gut. He leaned back against the building and took several deep breaths. It helped and the pain eased. Tuck counted his blessings, realizing how lucky he was that he hadn't messed up and done something to hurt the passengers. If the stage had tipped over, they'd all have been killed. He shook his head to rid himself of the image.

Within seconds he heard a crowd of people forming out front. They sounded like a flock of magpies after a picnic. He'd managed to get out of sight just in time. His experience as a detective taught him that being inconspicuous was necessary to do his job. When he got the chance, he'd talk it over with Mr. Hearst and if he had no objections, he'd report to the sheriff.

Tuck hugged the side of the building and worked his way to the corner where he could hear, but not be seen. The girl, Kelly, was telling someone about the holdup. He thought it strange, but kind of flattering that she seemed worried about him.

In order to get a better view, Tuck ducked down and quickly ran behind the building next door. From there he hugged the building as he moved toward the street and peeked around the corner. He was surprised to see the hack driver who was waiting at the junction talking to the sheriff. But he was even more surprised to see Kelly keep interrupting them. He wished he could hear what they were saying because she seemed to be very excited.

He watched as Kelly and the miners climbed aboard the hack and headed back the way the stage had come in. Then a stranger climbed aboard the empty stage and drove it up the street. He hoped the man was taking it to the livery stable. Those horses needed fresh water and a rubdown. Finally, almost as fast as it had formed, the crowd followed the sheriff as he took off in the same direction as the stage. When everyone was gone, Tuck was surprised to see his suitcase still standing on the platform. He quickly went to it, picked it up, and ducked back into the alley where he donned his hat and coat. Then, sticking to the alley, he headed in the opposite direction of the crowd.

He'd walked four or five minutes before he left the security of the alley and stepped out onto the main drag. The sound of a cracking whip made him look down Main Street where he spotted a slow-moving ten yoke of oxen pulling three heavily loaded wagons.

Tuck waited for the outfit to pass before working his way around the last wagon and walking up behind a short man swinging a long bullwhip. He followed for a few seconds and then said, "Excuse me, sir. Could you give me directions to Lead City?"

The bullwhacker turned and looked up. Tuck stared at the strange little man and held back the laugh in his throat. Above his waist, the man's body was as normal as his own, but his legs were extremely short and heavily bowed.

"Is that where you're heading for?" the little man asked.

"If so, throw your bag on one of the wagons. That's were I'm heading." He stuck out his hand. "Shorty is what most folks call me. Hope you don't mind a little palavering?"

Before they'd traveled a hundred yards, Tuck realized they were heading in a different direction than the one taken by the hack driver. He looked at Shorty, pointed down a street running off to their left, and said, "I was under the impression Lead City was that way."

Shorty nodded. "That's one way to go. I've got to make stops in Gayville and Central City. We'll enter Lead City from the opposite end of town. Won't take much longer and you'll get to see some of the country along Deadwood Creek."

Being short on options, Tuck acquiesced and tossed his bag on the first wagon before falling in alongside the whip-cracking little man. It was easy keeping up with the slow moving wagons, but putting up with Shorty's constant jabber was a different story. The only time he stopped telling stories was when they pulled into a mining camp called Gayville to drop off one of the wagons. In the better part of the hour it had taken to reach Gayville, Shorty had already given Tuck the lowdown on the freight business as well as the best saloons and history of every mining camp along the way.

Finally Tuck had had all he could stand. "I hate to interrupt you, but I didn't think it was going to take this long. Isn't there a faster way to get to Lead City?"

Shorty cracked his whip, sending an empty whiskey bottle flying from the road in front of the lead oxen's hooves. "Shouldn't rush things, young feller. But if you're that anxious, when we get to Central City I'll show you a shortcut. You'll have a tough climb though."

After several more minutes of Shorty's constant gibbering, they arrived in Central City. The camp consisted of a few wooden buildings constructed on the steep western slope of the gulch. All the buildings were dug into the hillside with their fronts supported on log pilings. A rough plank footbridge, suspended on long ropes, crossed Deadwood Creek from the hotel to a trail that snaked its way up the gulch's almost vertical eastern slope.

Shorty pointed at the mountain and said, "See that path?" Tuck nodded.

"It leads up to a mining camp called Terryville. When you get up there, ask anyone and they'll tell you how to get down into Lead City. Leave your bag on the wagon. I'll drop it off at the livery stable. They'll hold it for you."

Tuck pondered if he should trust the little man. He looked honest and for sure he couldn't wear any of Tuck's clothes. The mere thought of dragging that bag up the steep trail made up his mind for him. "Leaving the bag on the wagon seems like a good idea, but first I want to get something from it."

He climbed on the wagon wheel and unbuckled his suitcase. Then he quickly reached in and pulled out his navy Colt. He checked to make sure it was loaded, opened his shirt, and shoved the .45 in his waistband. Back on the ground, he said, "I'm much obliged to you." After shaking Shorty's hand, he smiled and said, "Maybe I'll see you in town. If I do, I'll buy you a drink."

Shorty returned the smile and said, "Be glad to take you up on that. Won't be pulling out till day after tomorrow. If you drop into the Silver Star Saloon, you'll probably find me." He let fly a jaw full of tobacco juice, cracked his whip, and went to drop off the supplies for Central City.

Halfway up the steep trail, Tuck realized he was either getting old, out of shape, or both. Each step took more effort. He looked up to where the trail crested the ridge and took a deep breath. The climb seemed to take forever, but less than twenty minutes later he crossed over the top.

On the other side, he found himself on the main drag of a fair-sized mining camp. In front of, according to the sign above the door, the Daisy Saloon, was a circle of six miners dressed in bib overalls, flannel shirts, and hobnailed boots. In the center of the circle, looking like a caged mountain lion, was a skinny, ebony-skinned man with snow-white hair. When the old man moved to escape, his unsteady gait made Tuck wonder if he was crippled or drunk. One of the miners held out his hand and offered a pint of whiskey to the captive and said, "You want this? Come and get it." Laughter filled the air above the circle.

The old man ignored the offer and tried to limp between two of the burly men. One of them grabbed his arm and spun him back into the center. The poor old guy didn't say a word, but the fear in his eyes caused Tuck's hair to bristle. He tried to escape again. As before, he was grabbed and pushed back into the circle.

This time, a curly-headed miner, the biggest one of the lot, stepped into the ring, put his boot in front of the old man's leg, and shoved. The poor old devil went facedown into the dirt. He remained still for a second, then struggled to get to his feet. The miner drew back his foot and kicked the old man in the ribs, causing him to grunt and curl up in a fetal position.

Tuck flinched as if he'd taken the kick himself. When the curly-headed miner started to give the old man another kick, Tuck saw red. Next thing he knew, he was straddling the groaning black man. He pointed his Colt at the miners and said, "If one of you bums makes a move, you're dead!"

The curly-headed bully scowled and said, "What are you, some kind of Yankee?"

Tuck pulled back the Colt's hammer. "All of you, just turn around and head up the hill."

Soon as the men moved away, Tuck reached down and pulled the old man to his feet. "Come on, Slim, we've got to get you out of here."

Up the street, the miners stopped, huddled in a group, and stared down on them. "You'll bloody well pay for that, pilgrim." Tuck turned and saw the barkeep from the Daisy Saloon. "That's the night shift from the Golden Terra. No matter how long it takes, they'll get even. You've sure stuck your neck out for a no-account Tom."

"I'm not afraid of a bunch of bullies," Tuck said. He put his hand under the old man's bony arm. "Come on friend, we'd better be going." Side by side they started down the trail to Lead City.

When they were out of sight of the miners, the old man turned to Tuck and said, "I sure thank you for sticking your neck out for me. But that bartender wasn't kidding, those miners won't rest till they get you."

Funny how different the old man sounded from most of the blacks Tuck had known. "I was thinking the same thing; guess I'll have to keep my guard up. By the way, my name is Tuck Powells. What's yours?"

The old man eased himself down on a tree stump, and said, "Ira Stewart." He offered his hand to Tuck.

Tuck gave the hand a gentle pump. It was like holding a fistful of bones. Tuck felt real compassion for the old man as he said, "How'd you get into that mess up there?" He jerked his head up the hill.

Ira paused for a second and said, "I guess I could blame it on this lame leg of mine. Whiskey eases the pain." He rubbed his right leg. "This morning some teamsters passed on their way to Terryville with a load of cordwood. I hitched a ride so I could replenish the bottle I'd finished earlier. I guess the miners wanted to have some fun with me. They sure do play rough."

"We'll get you another bottle when we get into town."

Tuck, looking down into a gulch formed by two steep mountain slopes, saw a developing town spreading along the bottom and up the sides. It had to be Lead City, but there was something about the place that didn't look right. Something was missing. Then it struck him that the slopes on both sides of the town were completely bare of trees. In their place stood thousands of tree stumps looking like tombstones in a giant graveyard. "What on earth happened to all the trees?" Tuck asked.

Ira grimaced as he struggled to stand up. When he finally made it, he said, "It takes a lot of wood to run a mine."

He pointed to their left where a portion of the tip of the mountain had been dug away. Hugh piles of cordwood were stacked between where they were standing and several long tin-sheeted buildings. "That's the Homestake," Ira said. "A rich man named George Hearst owns it. By the time he's done, he'll own all the mines in the area."

Tuck let the Hearst remark pass without comment as he took Ira's arm and helped him down the mountain. When he looked like he needed another rest, Tuck asked, "How did you hurt your leg?"

Ira stopped walking and said, "I was in the Union Army during the war and got to know General Custer. When the war ended, Custer made me his personal cook and brought me out west with the Seventh Calvary. In '69 he led an expedition into the Black Hills to look for white men and drive them out. The treaty had given all of the Black Hills to the Indians and they were complaining about the growing number of whites looking for gold."

They'd gone a few more steps, when Ira said, "We had a week or so to go before the expedition was scheduled to pull out. I was in camp getting the general's supper ready when we were attacked by a war party of Sioux. Next thing I knew a big buck came at me with a war axe. He swung. I ducked. He missed my head, but caught me in the knee, shattering my kneecap. One of the other troopers shot him before he had a chance to take another swing, but the damage was already done. I've hardly had a day without pain ever since."

Tuck saw the hurt in Ira's eyes. For some reason he knew he wasn't talking to the same helpless old cripple he rescued from the miners. He stared at the old man, and said, "Don't tell me Custer pulled out and left you behind?"

"Not at all," said Ira. "They put me on a wagon and took me to Fort Laramie. I was in the hospital for six months, but my wound was stubborn and wouldn't heal. Finally they offered me a discharge and a job in the stables." He smiled. "One night when I got fed up with the smell of horses, I walked out of the fort and headed for the hills. I've been here ever since. I guess because I wasn't white, the Indians left me alone. In fact, after a while we became friends and they made me one of them."

From the moment they started down the mountain, Tuck heard the steady drone of noises drifting up from the town. Stamp mills pounded. Compressors whined. Teamsters, hauling ore from the mines to the mills, cussed and yelled at their mules. Now that they were in Lead City, the streets were crowded with miners and other workmen. Dozens of new buildings were under construction. From the looks of it, a lot of people were going to get rich in this place.

The two men moved slowly through before they stopped in front of the Silver Star Saloon. While Ira waited outside, Tuck went in and bought a pint of whiskey and handed it to his new friend. "Here, maybe this will take the edge off that pain."

Ira looked around, then stuck the bottle under his shirt. "Hope I can pay you back someday. Why don't you come out and spend a few days at my cabin? It's probably the most beautiful country you'll ever see. If you've got a piece of paper, I'll draw you a map."

To humor the old man, Tuck pulled out a piece of paper and a pencil.

Ira eased himself down onto the edge of the wooden sidewalk and rested the paper on his good knee. Then, taking his time, he drew a professional-looking map, indicating landmarks, wagon roads, streams, and trails. When finished, he checked it over before handing it to Tuck. "My cabin is plenty big enough to hold visitors," he said.

Tuck bade good-bye to Ira and headed for a two-story building labeled Homestake Hotel. Inside the lobby, he approached the desk clerk and said, "I understand George Hearst resides here. I have a letter for him."

"You're in luck," said the clerk. "He's in the bar." He pointed to a stained-glass door on the opposite side of the lobby.

Inside the dimly lit, smoke-filled bar were several men seated at the six tables. Others stood at the bar. Tuck looked around the room trying to spot someone who fitted his image of a millionaire. Unable to do so, he asked the bartender, who pointed to a tall, muscular man wearing bib overalls and sporting a shaggy, tobacco-stained beard.

Tuck went to the man and said, "The bartender tells me you are George Hearst. I'm looking for the owner of the Homestake mine."

The man shifted his chaw of tobacco from one cheek to the other, then opened and closed his mouth a couple times before letting fly a glob of juice. A pinging sound echoed from the brass spittoon. "That's me," said the man. "I'm one of the owners. What can I do for you?"

Tuck took a paper from his pocket, and said, "I've got a letter from Mr. Tevis."

Hearst glanced down at the paper, picked up his bottle from the bar, poured a healthy shot of bourbon, and downed it in one gulp. He smacked his lips a couple of times, took the letter, and started reading it.

Tuck waited.

When Hearst finished reading, he looked at Tuck, laughed, and said, "Says here my partners sent you to make sure I don't get killed. I knew I should never have told those fools that someone was out to get me. Nevertheless they should know that I can take care of myself." He gave the paper back to Tuck. "Oh, well. You must be a good detective to work for Wells Fargo. I'll find something for you to do."

Hearst poured himself another shot and offered one to Tuck. Tuck refused. "I'll tell you what," Hearst said. "I had a contract crew of Cousin Jacks come in on this morning's stage. John, the lead man, told me that there was a one-eyed man asking a lot of questions about me and the Homestake."

Hearst pinged another shot of tobacco juice, then said, "First, take your time and find a place to stay. Soon as you're settled in, look around a bit and see if you can locate this guy. Try to find out what he's up to."

Tuck smiled and said, "I was on that stage. I know what he looks like and if you ask me he could be up to most anything."

Hearst's expression took on a quizzical look. "Are you the missing passenger John told me about? He said you disappeared, but he thought you got yourself killed in the holdup attempt."

Tuck was surprised that Hearst already knew what happened. "News sure travels fast. I'm the one who disappeared. But only because I didn't think it would a good idea to call attention to myself."

"Good move," Hearst said. "I'm the same way. Take your time and look me up when you've got something to report."

Chapter Four

After leaving George Hearst, Tuck went straight to the livery stable and picked up his bag. Then on advice of the hostler at the livery stable, he hurried down Main Street to a boardinghouse run by a Mrs. Robinson. "She's the best landlady in town," said the man.

The only room Mrs. Robinson had available was small, but very clean and neat. The feather bed, covered with a patchwork quilt, was comfortable and easily accommodated Tuck's long legs. There was also a washstand, a chest of drawers, and a cabinet to hang his coat and shirts. A tiny table and one chair were placed next to the small potbellied stove standing in the corner.

After Tuck stowed his gear, he sat down at the table to work out a plan of action. During the entire trip from San Francisco, Tuck had worried about how he was going to fulfill his mission. But after meeting George Hearst, the apprehension disappeared and he was confident that between him and Hearst they could handle almost anything. For sure Hearst wasn't worried and he looked like a tough old hombre who could hold his own.

A few minutes later, Tuck nonchalantly ambled into the Silver Star Saloon, took a seat at the bar, and ordered a beer. As the barkeep knifed the head off the glass, Tuck heard a commotion in the back. He turned to see was happening and spotted the one-eyed seaman trying to pull a black-haired girl down on his lap. Tuck's first thought was to go to her aid, but then she pulled free of the man's grasp and came running up to the bartender, and said, "If you don't do something about that slimy drunk, I'm walking out of here."

The bartender dropped the towel he was drying glasses with, moved to the end of the bar, ducked under the hinged flap, and charged toward the one-eyed seaman. The barkeep's wide back kept Tuck from hearing or seeing what was going on. However, when the barkeep turned around, he had the seaman by the arm and was marching him toward the door. All the way out, the drunken seaman mumbled incoherently, but offered no resistance.

Tuck paid for his untouched beer, went outside, and followed the seaman down Main Street. When, at the corner of Main and Mill, the seaman turned left, Tuck was close behind. Halfway down the block, the seaman staggered between two buildings and into a back alley. Tuck caught up just in time to see him enter a door to the building on his right.

While wondering if he should also go through the door, Tuck leaned against the rough planking of a storage shed and lit a smoke. A steady drone of laughter, loud talk, and music drifted out of the watched building. After a minute, Tuck decided he'd just wait for the seaman to come back out.

He'd been waiting for about ten minutes when he heard the muffled crack of a pistol shot. He straightened up, dropped his smoke, and snuffed it out with the toe of his boot. Suddenly the door opened a crack, remained that way for a second, and then swung open. Framed in the doorway was a beat-up-looking Kelly Ryan. She paused for a moment, then jumped down the flight of three steps and ran toward him. As she got closer, he saw the wild look on her face.

Tuck stepped from his hiding place and Kelly ran straight into his arms. Immediately she tried to pull away. When Tuck held on, she started beating violently on his chest. Tuck took a firmer grip on her shoulders, held her at arms length, and said, "Take it easy, Kelly. It's me, Tuck Powells."

She looked up through glazed-over eyes, blinked, and then said, "Mr. Powells! Thank goodness you're alive."

With her body shivering like a quaking ash leaf, she started sobbing uncontrollably. After several seconds, she settled down enough to say, "Oh, Tuck. I just killed a man. I've got to get away from this horrible place. I just have to get away."

Trying to calm her violent shivering, Tuck wrapped his sheepskin jacket around her shoulders. Then he took her by the arm and together they rushed up the slope toward Terryville.

By the time they came to a large stack of cordwood, they were both gasping for air. On the woodpile's blind side, they fell to the ground and for several seconds fought to catch their breath. Finally Tuck said, "We should be safe here for a little while. Now tell me what happened."

She looked as if she was going to talk, but instead started laughing hysterically. Tuck tried his best to calm her, but she wouldn't stop. Finally, unsure of what else to do, he shook her roughly and said, "Kelly, if you keep this up, I can't help you."

She stopped immediately, took a deep breath, held it for a minute, and said, "Do you have a handkerchief?"

By this time Tuck was totally confused, but he handed her his red kerchief and watched as she wiped her eyes and blew her nose.

Then feeling a need to do something, he took her chin and raised it to where they were staring into each other's eyes. Pangs of pity pounded his heart as he said, "Are you sure the man you shot was the same man who was on the stage with us?"

Kelly nodded.

Tuck sighed. At least his first assignment was completed. The one-eyed man wouldn't be causing Mr. Hearst any trouble. Now he needed a place for Kelly to hide. He gently put his arm around her shoulders. She pressed closer against him and didn't try to remove it.

For more than an hour they remained hidden behind the woodpile. With Kelly sheltered in his arm, Tuck thought of Mary Lou and pictured how she must've hoped for someone to come to her aid, but she wasn't so lucky.

When he couldn't come up with anything else, Tuck said, "I'm going to take you to the boardinghouse I'm living in. Mrs. Robinson is a nice lady and I'm sure she'll understand and maybe she can recommend a safe place for you stay."

By sticking to the shadows and moving a few feet at a time, they slowly worked their way back down the hill to Lead City. When they finally arrived at the boardinghouse, Kelly hid in the outhouse while Tuck went inside to talk to Mrs. Robinson.

Inside, he gently knocked on his landlady's door. When she answered, Tuck quickly gave her a brief rundown and asked for her help. Tuck realized she was really concerned when she said, "We can't let Charley Utter get her. He's a bad one and will kill her for sure. Bring her in here, we'll figure something out."

When Mrs. Robinson saw the large purple bruise on the right side of Kelly's face and the cut above her left eye, she said, "You poor dear. What have they done to you?" She reached out and took Kelly in her arms. "You must be freezing in that skimpy outfit. We've got to get you something to wear." She quickly went to her closet and removed a yellow robe she handed to Kelly. "For now you can slip into this."

She turned to Tuck and said, "You turn around and let Kelly take off those rags and put on the robe." After helping Kelly button up, she said, "I think we all need a cup of coffee. I'll get the pot. You two stay put."

Tuck stared at Kelly. What a shame. A few hours ago she was a beautiful redhead and now she was a battered shell of her former self. He knew he was taking on a huge task, but he couldn't abandon her. Not like this. He had to make sure she was safe.

But that was not his job; he was hired to keep Mr. Hearst safe. How on earth could he do both jobs at the same time?

Kelly must have read his mind; she put her hand on his arm and said, "I hate to trouble you, Tuck, but I don't think I can survive this awful place by myself. Please help me till I can raise the money to get me back to San Francisco."

Tuck smiled and gently squeezed her fingers. "Don't you worry. I won't let anyone hurt you, but I hope Mrs. Robinson knows of some place you can go. I sure don't know of one."

Kelly wiped some tears from her eyes and said, "Trixie told me that if I got away I should go to Mrs. Hayes in Deadwood. She said she's an old woman who looks out for girls in trouble."

They both tensed at the two quick taps on the door. Mrs. Robinson entered carrying a large serving tray holding a heaping plate of doughnuts, a steaming pot of coffee, two cups and saucers, along with milk and sugar. "Have some of these," she said. "You'll both feel better. While you're eating, I'll get dressed." With her slippers shuffling across the floor, she disappeared behind a black lacquered Chinese privacy screen.

When she came out, she was wearing a white long-sleeved blouse and a long skirt. Her hair was tied in a bun. Compared to Kelly she was a homely woman, but her eyes were full of kindness.

"Do you know anything about a Mrs. Hayes in Deadwood?" asked Tuck.

Mrs. Robinson's grim expression brightened. "Why, yes. I should have thought of her. She just might be the one to keep Kelly safe. They call her the Mother of the Badlands."

"But how will I get to Deadwood?" Kelly asked.

Mrs. Robinson put her arm around Kelly and said, "Hush now and let me think. First of all, you've got to have something to wear. If I remember right, I've still got one of my son's suits. You don't mind dressing like a boy, do you?"

"I'll do whatever it takes."

Soon as Mrs. Robinson left the room, Kelly stared at Tuck for a second, then asked, "You won't leave me, will you?"

"Of course not. I'll stay with you till I'm sure you're safe."

"Will you help me get back to San Francisco?"

Tuck bit his bottom lip watching the look in Kelly's green eyes. "I sure will," he said.

A few minutes later, Mrs. Robinson came back with an armful of clothes. "They're a mite wrinkled from the trunk, but I'm pretty sure they'll fit. Go behind the screen and try them on." She shifted her attention to Tuck. "You stay here with her. I'll go to the livery stable and get my buckboard and then I'll drive you down to Deadwood."

Before Tuck could say a word, Mrs. Robinson was out the door. Again, he thought of Mary Lou. If only someone had been there to help her, maybe she'd still be alive. The thought suddenly made him feel better about what he was doing. He swore that he'd not let any more harm come to Kelly.

When she emerged from behind the screen, Tuck hardly recognized her. She was dressed in a black suit, white shirt, and black tie. On her feet were black shoes, and covering her red hair was a flat-crowned hat. She looked almost exactly like a Pennsylvania Amish boy from Tuck's home county.

"The shoes are a little big," Kelly said. "But everything else fits fine. How do I look?"

Tuck chuckled. "Just like a boy after a schoolyard fight."

When Mrs. Robinson returned they were downing the last of the doughnuts. "Are you ready?" she asked.

Tuck took Kelly's hand and they followed Mrs. Robinson out the back door to where the buckboard stood waiting. The three of them climbed on board with Kelly squeezed between Mrs. Robinson and Tuck. "You'd better drive, Tuck," said Mrs. Robinson. "Someone might wonder why a woman's driving a man and boy through town."

Tuck nodded and took the reins. Then following Mrs. Robinson's directions, he took the high-stepping bay through Lead City's back alleys and onto the road running down Gold Run Gulch to Deadwood. "How will we find Mrs. Hayes?" he asked.

"You won't have any trouble," she answered. "She sells fruit on Main Street. You'll recognize her stand by its red awning. Behind it is the clapboard shack she lives in. I'm sure she'll still be out front; she never closes before the saloons do."

Tuck flicked the reins across the horse's rump. They moved at a steady pace down the narrow gulch till they reached the outskirts of Deadwood. Mrs. Robinson reached across Kelly and tapped Tuck's arm. "Better pull up here and get off. Just walk over to Main Street and make a right. You'll recognize the place when you see it. Make sure you keep in touch. I'll be dying to know what's going on."

Main Street was crowded with people, most of them in varying stages of drunkenness. Tuck was glad. A man and boy wouldn't stand out in this crowd.

Kelly spotted the stand first. Sure enough, under a bright red awning, an unkempt old woman sat in a large wooden rocker. Her eyes were closed and she looked sound asleep. They stepped under the awning and Tuck said, "Mrs. Hayes?"

Without noticeably opening her eyes, the old lady said, "You want to buy an apple for the boy?"

Tuck gently positioned Kelly in front of him, and said,

"This is a young lady. Her name is Kelly Ryan and she needs help. Charley Utter is looking for her and she has nowhere to go."

The old lady shook her head. "That Charley Utter is bad news. If he finds out I've got her here, he'll make real trouble for me."

Kelly kneeled beside Mrs. Hayes and said, "If you can just help me tonight, I'll try to leave tomorrow."

Mrs. Hayes cupped Kelly's chin in her old weathered hand. "Shucks, girl. I didn't say I wouldn't help you. Go to my house back there and find yourself a place to sleep. Try not to wake the children."

Kelly looked at Tuck.

He nodded and said, "Do as Mrs. Hayes says. I'm going to get a room at the Custer Hotel. I'll be back first thing in the morning and we'll plan our next move."

When he saw Kelly enter the house, Tuck turned and went back up Main Street. In the Custer Hotel, he booked a room, undressed, and fell into bed where he lay back on his pillow with his hands clasped behind his head. Tuck knew he'd taken on a tough job, but for the first time since Mary Lou's funeral, he felt really needed.

Chapter Five

Somewhere ensnarled in the mixed-up dream he was having, a bell was ringing. Tuck opened his eyes to darkness. Where was he? The bell continued without letup. Then it came to him. He was in the Custer Hotel, and the sound was a clamoring fire bell!

He jumped from his bed, rushed to the window, and lifted the shade. On the other side of the creek behind the hotel, several buildings were ablaze. Flames danced high into the air and looked like it was spreading fast by wind carrying sparks and embers toward Main Street. Even though thick smoke blanketed the area, flames illuminated the open space behind the hotel.

Tuck juggled from one leg to the other as he struggled to don his pants and boots. Then, while working his way into his shirt and coat, he ran into the hall and bounded down the back stairs. Outside, the bell, echoing between the buildings, was even louder. The night was alive with sound and fire.

"Oh, my Lord!" someone cried. "The whole town is on fire."

Whooom! A gigantic explosion of fire and wind knocked Tuck to the ground. His eyes wouldn't focus. His ears rang. He moved gingerly. Nothing seemed broken. Kelly! He fought to get to his feet. When he finally found his balance, he started running toward Main Street only to be stopped by three men dragging a pumper toward the creek. Seeing a chance to help stop the spread of the fire, he joined the three men.

When they got to the center of the stream, they dropped an intake pipe into the shallow water. Two of the men, unrolling the hose as they ran, rushed toward the burning buildings. Tuck and the other man grabbed the pump handles and started pumping. It was several pumps before water started gushing from the nozzle. The cool liquid caused the burning wood to hiss and spit. But after a few minutes, the flow slowed to a trickle. The intake was clogged. The creek was too shallow.

The other pump handler yelled, "Durn this cheap town. We'll never be able to beat this fire. Let's get out of here."

The fire was getting hotter. Tuck felt tightness in his chest and his mouth was bone dry. The backs of the buildings facing Main Street were bathed in a ruddy glow from their windows reflecting the flames leaping skyward. Small fires burned on some of the roofs. In a matter of minutes, Main Street would be in flames. He had to get to the fruit stand. Kelly would be waiting for him.

Before he took a dozen steps, another explosion froze Tuck in his tracks. As he turned to look, he spotted sparks flying from the rubble of a collapsed building.

Suddenly he heard a scream. Who was that? He held his breath hoping he could hear better. "H-e-l-l-l-p!" It was coming from his left. Someone was trapped. Tuck sprinted in the direction of the cries.

It was hard seeing in the thick smoke, but then Tuck spotted the caller. It was a man lying on the ground, one leg pinned under a large beam. Tuck reached for the burning beam. It was too hot to touch. The heat was unbearable;

his lungs burned. He ran back to the creek and quickly rolled in the shallow water. When soaked to the skin he pulled a rail off a fence, ran back to the man, stuck one end of the rail under the blazing beam, and rolled it off the man's leg. Tuck threw down the rail, grabbed the man's overall straps, and dragged him to the creek. Steam and the smell of burning flesh rose from the man's body. Tuck stared at the man's blackened face, and said, "Can you walk? We've got to get out from between these buildings."

The man held out his hand. "If you help me, I'll make it." With Tuck's assistance the man struggled to his feet and held tight to Tuck's shoulder as they trekked lopsidedly toward Main Street. The intense heat and fire crackled as it licked up the rapidly depleting fresh air. Out of the thick smoke, bits of fire flew in every direction. After slowly working their way through a narrow alley, they came out on Main Street.

Tuck stepped into the street and flagged down an approaching buckboard and convinced the driver to take on a passenger. He'd no sooner helped the burned man climb aboard when the nervous driver cracked his whip and the buckboard sped up Deadwood Gulch.

With that problem out of the way, Tuck looked around at the people milling about in confusion. No one seemed to be doing anything to put out the fire. Deadwood's normally boisterous residents looked as if they were waiting for some mystic guidance from above.

In front of the Gem Theater, a group of people watched a scantily clad woman with long black hair stagger from one side of the second story balcony to the other. The blank look in her eyes made Tuck believe she was in some sort of a stupor, probably from opium. Suddenly she stopped pacing and threw a leg over the rail. Obviously she was going to jump, but why? The theater wasn't burning. Tuck yelled, "Stay where you are; I'll come up and help you down."

He couldn't tell if she understood, but he didn't have

time to repeat it. He ran to the front door. It was locked. He tried the windows and found them also locked. He picked up a stone, smashed the glass, and climbed inside where he found himself in a long room filled with table and chairs. A stage ran across one end.

Spotting the stairs to the second floor, Tuck ran up and started pounding on doors. Surprisingly the place was full of people, most of them drunk and half-asleep. He tried the door that he figured should lead to the woman's room. It was locked. He raised his foot and kicked it in. He was too late. The woman was no longer on the balcony. He rushed to the rail and looked down. She was sprawled facedown on the dusty street without a soul helping her. He went back into the room, stripped a sheet from the bed, and tossed it down to one of the gawking people. "Here, cover her up." A woman dressed in fringed buckskins helped her to her feet, wrapped the sheet around her, and led her away.

Tuck looked around again. Adam's Grocery was now burning. Forks of flame had climbed one wall and part of the roof. It was only a matter of time before the entire city was aflame. Time was running out. He had to get to Kelly.

He climbed over the rail, hung by his hands for a second, and then dropped to the street. He'd no sooner started running toward the fruit stand when he was stopped again. This time it was a burning hay wagon being hung up by a hitching post lodged between a wheel and the wagon bed. A team of wild-eyed horses struggled to break free, but the more they panicked, the tighter they became ensnarled.

Tuck ducked between the rearing horses and grabbed a bridle in each hand. He yelled for help and two men jumped from the sidewalk to lend a hand. Tuck told the two men, "Each of you grab a bridle and try to hold them while I cut them loose." He opened his Barlow knife and sliced through the leather traces. "Let 'em go," he said, then watched the frightened horses speeding down Main Street with their reins and tattered harness straps flapping across their backs.

When he finally reached the fruit stand, the red awning was burning in two places. Tuck rushed to the shack where Kelly was staying. It was still intact. With no time for formalities, he hit the door with his shoulder. The wood splintered and the door flew from its hinges. A lamp burned dimly on the kitchen table. The two rooms were filled with women and children. No wonder they called Mrs. Hayes the Mother of the Badlands.

Then he saw Kelly, still in her boy's suit, curled up in a corner. He started toward her but was stopped short by Mrs. Hayes pointing a shotgun at him. "Mrs. Hayes!" he said as he threw up his hands. "The whole town's on fire! We've got to get out of here."

Smoke poured through the open door. Mrs. Hayes lowered the shotgun and leaned it in a corner. "Come on, ladies," she said. "We're going to take the children for a walk." Her voice was calm without a hint of panic.

Tuck dashed to Kelly's side. She looked dazed. "Don't be afraid. There's a bad fire outside. We're leaving now." He took her hand and pulled her to her feet. "Don't worry, we'll be fine."

Through trembling lips she said, "Oh, Tuck, I really must be bad luck. Everything has gone wrong since we left Cheyenne. I should've stayed in San Francisco; everyone would've been better off."

He gazed at the battered young woman dressed in boy's clothing and wondered what happened to the spitfire he'd first encountered. "You can't blame yourself, Kelly. This is a tough part of the world. Things happen here that don't happen in other places. Come on now, we've got to get a move on."

Outside, all of Main Street was engulfed in flames. Their only chance was to climb the almost vertical slope behind the shack. Mrs. Hayes would be a problem. She was grossly overweight and could hardly walk, let alone climb a mountain. But she couldn't be left behind.

Tuck started the other women and children toward the

top of the hill. Then, one step at a time, he and Kelly helped Mrs. Hayes up the steep incline. It was exhausting work. Every five or six steps they had to stop and rest.

By the time they reached the top and found a level spot where the others were waiting, dawn was breaking in the eastern sky. Kelly and Mrs. Hayes sat down to rest. Tuck was staring at the gulch below when he felt that familiar tug on his sleeve.

"What are we going to do now?" Kelly asked. "We can't stay here."

Tuck shook his head. Fate had dealt him a hand to play—he couldn't throw in till the final card was dropped. He gently squeezed her hand as he said, "We'll leave the others here and keep going. I need time to think."

Chapter Six

Archibald Bowlan, owner of the Father DeSmet mine, leaned back in his chair and stared at the ceiling as he said, "Way I hear it, the fire started in the Star Bakery then spread to Jensen and Bliss's hardware store. Unfortunately Jensen had eight kegs of gunpowder in his storeroom. Soon as the flames reached the powder it exploded and blew the store to smithereens. Embers scattered all over town. When it was over, more than three hundred buildings went up in smoke—even those new buildings that were supposed to be fireproof. The builders hadn't taken into account that an explosion could open cracks in the bricks allowing the fire to get inside."

Bowlan straightened up then leaned forward, studying the faces of the six men seated around the Executive Dining Room table of the DeSmet boardinghouse. Bowlan had called the meeting to fill his partners in on the progress of their battle against George Hearst and the Homestake. He pointed to an empty chair, and said, "Where's Hank Young? He said he'd stick with us."

Bill Lardner, one of the owners of the Mammoth mine,

hesitated, then said, "Hank won't be here. Hearst offered him ten thousand for his claim and Hank grabbed it."

Bowlan threw his arms in the air, shook his head, and then started pounding on the white tablecloth as he said, "I knew this was going to happen. I told you before that if we're going to stop Hearst, we've got to stick together. That old son of a polecat is out to get his hands on every claim in the district and if he has to, he'll pick us off one by one." With that said, he plopped back in his chair and pulled out a long, black cigar. "I need something to calm my nerves," he said as he bit off the tip. He took a match from his pocket and struck it on the bottom of his chair. Archie held the stogie in the flame for a couple of seconds before he stuck it in his mouth and started puffing. Clouds of smoke rose to engulf the oil-fed chandeliers hanging above their heads.

With the tip glowing cherry-red, Bowlan took the cigar from his mouth, looked around the table, and said, "I've got more bad news. The guy I brought in from 'Frisco to take care of Hearst got himself killed. One of Charley Utter's girls shot him in the head." He paused to let his words sink in and to catch their reactions before saying, "Worst part is, I'd already paid him for the job. I hate to admit it, but it looks as if we've bought ourselves a bad deal."

Willie Schnitzel, a bearded man in a slouch hat, slowly rose to his feet and said, "I'm glad it happened. I've had a hard time sleeping since I teamed up with this bunch. George Hearst may be a money-hungry old buzzard, but he stays within the law and I don't want any part of killing him. As a matter of fact, if he offers me a fair price for the Deadwood mine, I'm going to let him have it." He stepped back, slid his chair under the table, and left the room.

Archie Bowlan was livid. "Any more of you cowards want to pull out? If so, do it now. I'm going to fight Hearst down to the wire, and I'm going to do it with or without the rest of you. But I'm sure you all realize that Hearst's got a load of money behind him and the more we stick together, the better our chances."

Homer Lyman, a trim man with his dark-brown hair parted on the side, stood up and removed his red mackinaw from the back of his chair. "You can count me out. Hearst has already offered me a down payment of sixteen hundred bucks for the Golden Star. I think I'll take him up on it." He then followed Schnitzel out the door.

"Anyone else?" Bowlan said, looking straight at Jack Phillips, the oldest member of the group.

Phillips, a lean, tired-looking man with gray eyes, returned Bowlan's stare. While maintaining eye contact, he too got up from his chair, coughed to clear his throat, and in a calm measured voice said, "I want to tell all of you something. I shouldn't have joined up with you in the first place. Hearst is one of us. I worked with him on the American River in California and again on the Comstock. Maybe he's smarter than us, or maybe he's just luckier than us, but he never cheated or tried to get something for nothing." He then took out his pipe, lit it with a lucifer, and puffed till he had a cloud of smoke rising above. "Now that I've finally got a mine, I sure don't want to give it away, but I'm too old to start a long court battle." He took a couple more puffs before saying, "Time after time the claims in this district have been staked, filed, and sold with different configurations. I'm not sure if any one of us, including Hearst, can say for sure he's got a legal claim. That means court fights or selling out to the highest bidder."

The old man scratched his stubble-covered chin, then said, "Like I said, I'm too old to fight, so I'm going to offer Hearst the Highland for twenty thousand. If any of you can top that, start talking."

When no one made an offer, Phillips put on his hat, knocked the fire from his pipe, and with his rubber boots scraping along the floor, shuffled out.

"I never was sure of him," Bowlan said. "Now there's just the four of us. It's probably better this way. The more people involved, the more likely our plans will get in the wrong hands. If you guys want, I'll look for someone else to knock off Hearst."

Captain Huron, owner of the Old Abe, shifted in his chair as he said, "Before we get into that, I'd like to know if we're going to let that little harlot get away with our money?"

A chorus of "yeas" came from around the table.

Bowlan shook his heavily jowled head. "Well, I'm not sure if the girl got away with the money or if Charley Utter lifted it when he found the body. We can try to find the girl, but I'm too smart to take on Utter. Of course, if any of you want to try it, the rest of us won't stop you."

The Mammoth's Bill Lardner stood up, ran his fingers through his long red hair, and said, "Let's face it—the money's gone. As for the other business, I don't think it'll do a durn bit of good to kill Hearst. His partners will just send someone else, and you can bet they'll send an army of Wells Fargo police along with him. What we need is a good lawyer." The others nodded in agreement.

General Gashwiler slapped the table so hard it sent an echo throughout the room. "Blast the lawyers! A gun's the only thing that'll stop Hearst."

Lardner waited for him to calm down before saying, "Take it easy, General. I'll tell you why we need a lawyer. A big chunk of the Homestake crosses my claim and if I can prove first ownership in court, Hearst's claim will be invalid. That'll stop him in his tracks."

Captain Huron smiled and said, "Good idea, Bill. Part of my claim overlaps the Giant and Hearst needs the Giant. If I can get undisputed title to my claim, it'll put another roadblock in his way."

Archie Bowlan put a big smile on his face as he stood up and said, "Gentlemen, what we need right now is some refreshments. I'm going to step out and see what the cook can scrape together."

Gashwiler, a tall military-postured man and owner of the

Caledonia, waited till Bowlan stepped out before he said, "Maybe we shouldn't hire someone to get rid of Hearst, but if the old coot happened to get drunk and fall down a shaft, we'd all be better off."

Lardner met Gashwiler's gaze and said, "Won't argue that, General, but we've got to make sure we get a lawyer that can do the job. I don't think any of us has any more money to throw away."

Suddenly the door opened and Archie Bowlan entered carrying a bottle of bourbon and four whiskey glasses. On his heels came a mahogany-skinned woman with her black hair rolled up in a bun carrying a tray of half-moon shaped pasties. Bowlan set down his tray, turned to the woman, and said, "Men, I want you to meet Aunt Lou Marshbanks. Some of you may have seen her at the Wagner. I stole her from them and have made her the DeSmet's executive chef."

The woman gave the men a look that told them she wasn't buying Bowlan's line of bull. She set her platter on the table and left the room without saying a word.

Bowlan stuck out his chest. "Wait till you taste these pasties. They're much better than the ones made by the Cousin Jennies. Aunt Lou says it's in the crust. She uses butter instead of lard." He picked up one of the meat-and-potato pies, took a large bite, and washed it down with a shot of bourbon. "That's what I call good eating." He smacked his lips. "While I was out, I took the liberty of sending a messenger for Pat Flavin. Pat's a top-notch attorney. He knows mining law like Aunt Lou knows victuals. Besides, he's got connections."

A few minutes later, a knock on the door sent Bowlan rushing across the room. Framed in the doorway stood a bulky, red-faced man wearing a brown suit with checkered vest. A heavy gold watch chain crossed his belly.

Bowlan grabbed the man's hand and said, "Pat. Glad you could make it. I've already told these gentlemen about you." Bowlan looked around the table. "Any objections to putting Pat on the payroll?" When no one answered, Bowlan said, "Looks as if you're our man. Come on in."

Flavin took a seat at the table. Then without waiting for an invitation, he grabbed a pastie, gulped it down, belched, rubbed his belly, and reached for another one. "Best pastie I ever ate," he said. "Think I'll have another one."

Archie Bowlan chuckled. "Pat, the way you down those pasties you'd think you was a Cousin Jack."

Pat put the pastie back and said, "Now, I understand you fellas want me to stop George Hearst from taking control of the district?"

There was a nodding of heads.

"Well, first I'll jot down a few notes, then see what has to be done. When I'm ready, I'll tell Archie and he'll call another meeting."

With business finished for now, Archie held the door while his guests left. Pat Flavin waited till everyone else was out the door before grabbing the pastie he'd put down and took it with him.

Chapter Seven

After saying good-bye to Mrs. Hayes and the others, Tuck took Kelly's arm and they worked their way along the ridge till they came to an outcropping of rock. The climb to the top of the formation left them out of breath and near exhaustion. On the edge of the rim rock, they sat down to catch their breath. They rested a few minutes then Tuck eased his way to the edge and looked down. The wind had lessened and the fire was burning itself out. As near as he could tell, the entire business district, including his hotel, was gutted. Nothing but smoldering skeletons of buildings remained.

Across the gulch, hundreds of people like themselves were taking refuge from the fire. Also like themselves, several people were clustered on top of a reddish-brown rock formation. Another group had climbed even higher and was perched on a series of huge white cliffs. It was obvious that a lot of people were going to be looking for a place to sleep that night.

Tuck reached into his pocket for his tobacco pouch and

came across Ira's map. He was studying it when Kelly asked, "What's that?"

"It's a map. When I was first trying to get to Lead City, I helped an old soldier out of a jam. In gratitude he invited me to visit him at his cabin in the wilderness. To make it easier for me, he drew me a map. Only trouble is this map starts out from Lead City, and for sure we can't go there."

Kelly gave him a quizzical look as she said, "Are we going to his cabin?"

Tuck sighed. "I can't think of anywhere else to go. I'm pretty sure Ira will take care of you till I find a way to safely get you out of the Black Hills."

"You're going to leave me alone with a strange man?" she asked. "I'm not sure I want that."

Tuck smiled and put his arm around her. He was surprised how good it felt as he said, "Ira's a nice old soldier. He'll give you no problem. I liked him from the moment I met him and I know you will too."

"But how are we going to get there?"

"We'll have to walk. It'll probably take a couple of days, but with Charley Utter and the sheriff hunting you, we can't risk going to town for a buggy."

"But do you think you can find the way? You said the map starts in Lead City. Isn't that a long way from here?"

Tuck held the paper so she could look at it. He put his finger on the map and said, "See Terry Peak here? If we were going from Lead it would be on our right. If we go the way I'm thinking of, it'll be on our left." He pointed to another spot. "This is Spearfish Canyon. We'll get down in the canyon floor and follow the creek upstream." His finger moved again. "When we get to this string of beaver dams, we'll know exactly where we're at and should have no trouble finding the cabin."

Doubt still showed in her eyes, but he didn't know what else to say to make her believe his words. "Let's get going," he said. "We'll walk along the ridge so we can follow

Deadwood Creek." He folded up the map and started walking. Kelly watched for a second, then hurried to catch up.

For six hours they kept a steady routine. They walked for a half hour, then stopped for a few minutes to catch their breath. At each stop, Kelly replaced the moss Tuck had given her to fill the space behind her heels in the too-large shoes. It helped some, but not enough to prevent the nasty blisters now adorning both heels.

With great effort and trying patience they worked their way in and out of one brush-filled gully after another. Some were deep and narrow. Others were nothing more than dips in the ground. Between the gullies they moved through acres of tall pines interspersed with droves of aspen and birch. Most of the steep slopes were covered with thick deadfalls and huge boulders. Every once in a while Tuck climbed a tree to make sure Terry Peak was where he thought it should be. As near as he could tell, they were going in the right direction.

On the edge of a grass-filled meadow, Tuck motioned for Kelly to stop. In a stand of birch on the opposite side of the meadow were three beautiful whitetail deer, a small buck and two does. When Tuck raised his hand to point at a larger buck standing further back in the trees, all four bounded into flight with their white flags signaling their farewells.

After working their way down a thicker than usual deadfall-strewn slope, they came to a rutted wagon road. "Let's stop here for a minute," Tuck said as he stared in both directions. "I wonder where this road will take us?"

Without answering, Kelly limped down the bank of the small stream running alongside the road and plopped down on a large rock. She then removed her shoes and stuck her blistered feet in the cold water. "This feels good," she said as she splashed in the clear water. "I'm getting hungry. What are we going to eat?"

Tuck, also feeling hunger pangs, said, "I think we're pretty safe for now. I'll look for some berries or maybe try to catch us a fish. But I'm really wondering if this road leads to a mining camp. If it does, I can buy some supplies." He shaded his eyes with his hand as he peered into the distance. "It looks as if it might. Do you suppose we should follow it and see what happens?"

Kelly gave him a funny look, and said, "You really want my opinion?"

"Sure I do. We're in this together, aren't we?"

Kelly's eyes lit up and a smile spread across her face. "I think I'll let you decide what we should do. But if it's alright with you, I'm walking barefoot for a while."

Tuck returned her smile. Kelly was a tough cookie and Tuck was becoming more attached to her with every passing minute. "Watch where you step," he said. "We've got to keep moving."

They followed the road for twenty minutes or so when they came face-to-face with a little old man leading a shaggy brown burro. The man's head was all hair and beard topped by an old, floppy-brimmed hat. In the midst of all the hair, a pair of bright blue eyes showed through gold-rimmed spectacles resting on a sunburned, button nose. "Howdy, folks," he said. "My name is Johnny. You two sure don't look like you belong out here in the middle of nowhere."

Tuck stuck out his hand. "I'm Tuck Powells," he said. "And this is my nephew, Kelsey. We were in Deadwood till the whole town burned down and we lost everything. We're trying to find work. Can you tell us where this road leads?"

"Sure can, cousin. I knew there was a fire burning somewhere but I thought it was a forest fire. So you say it was Deadwood? Well, Deadwood wasn't much good for nothing but gamblin' and drinkin' anyway." He giggled like a little kid. "Now you want to know where you're heading?" He paused. When Tuck didn't answer, the little man said, "I'll start by telling you that you are standing in the middle of Nevada Gulch. This road will take you to a mining camp called Trojan. There's not much there but a general store, a saloon, and a boardinghouse. Don't know if the mine is hiring but you can give it a try."

Johnny then removed his battered hat and scratched his head. "Now if you want to scamper over this mountain here"—pointing to the left—"you'll find a bigger place called Terry. There's a couple of mines there and one of them should be looking for workers." He tugged the rope tied to his heavily loaded burro, and said, "Come on, Susie, we've got some pannin' to do over on Potato Creek."

The old prospector led his burro in the direction they'd just came from. Skinny ankles showed below the legs of his baggy britches. Both elbows stuck out of his threadbare shirt.

Kelly looked at Tuck and said, "What a strange little man. Have you decided which camp we will head for?"

Thinking of the last time a little man told him to climb over a mountain, Tuck said, "We're going to follow this road to the place he called Trojan. He said there was a store where I can buy some food and find out how to get to Spearfish Canyon."

Kelly touched Tuck's arm and said, "I don't want to be a bother, but do you suppose you can buy me something to put on these blisters?"

"I'll see what they have," Tuck said.

Close to an hour later they rounded a bend in the road and found themselves standing in front of a log building with a porch running the full front. Above the porch hung a sign reading *General Store*. On the deck of the porch stood a couple of straight-back chairs, a wooden box full of axe and pick handles, a pile of dried codfish, and several unopened crates.

Tuck took the two steps in one leap, then turned and held out his hand to Kelly. "Why don't you take one of those chairs and rest your feet? I'll go inside and get what we need."

Coming in from the bright sunlight, it took Tuck's eyes

a few seconds to adjust to the dimly lighted interior. The place was wall-to-wall clutter. Overstocked shelves, tables, and counters were piled high with merchandise. Picks and shovels leaned against the walls. Coils of various-sized rope and wire hung from the overhead beams. The air was permeated with the odors of coffee, onions, smoked hams, bacon, peppers, tobacco, beeswax, and leather for making boots, saddles and harness, all vying for dominance. On the counter, next to an open bottle of whiskey, stood a scale for weighing gold dust. Behind the scale stood an overweight, bald-headed man.

The man came from behind the counter, wiped his hands on his apron, and said, "What can I do for you, Mister?"

Tuck shook the man's hand then ordered a coffeepot, frying pan, blankets, and enough food for at least three days. Hopefully it'd hold them till they got to the cabin. Then Tuck remembered and said, "My nephew's outside with some blistered feet. Can you sell me something to help him out?"

The clerk nodded, went to an out-of-the-way shelf, and came back with a pair of boy's heavy wool socks, a tin of carbolic salve, and a roll of gauze bandage. "These should do the trick," he said.

While the clerk wrapped the order in brown paper, Tuck picked out a penny's worth of peppermint sticks. The order came to a little less than nine dollars. Tuck paid with a ten-dollar gold piece. He pocketed his change, picked up the package, and started for the door. He hadn't taken three steps when he turned back to the clerk, and asked, "I almost forgot. What's the best way to get to Spearfish Canyon? I hear the fishing is great." He listened to the clerk's instructions and went outside.

Chapter Eight

The giant, scraggly-faced man staggered out of the saloon and headed up the path toward the store. Just looking at him made Kelly remember the hundreds of times she had seen her father come home in the same condition. He looked in her direction, an evil glare in his eyes. He started toward her. She slipped her aching feet into her shoes.

From the path he mumbled something so slurred she couldn't understand a word. He kept coming. When he started climbing the stairs to the porch she was ready to bolt. Suddenly the door opened and Tuck stepped out.

The man's eyes got as big as pie plates. He let go a string of angry, unintelligible words obviously directed at Tuck. Tuck seemed to recognize the miner who was about the same height as he was, but the man's huge arms and shoulders dwarfed Tuck's in comparison. He stopped and with difficulty forming his words, said, "What'd ya do, trade that black devil for a kid?" He shook his fist at Tuck. "I'll get you now for pulling that hogleg on me and my boys."

The miner lunged forward. Tuck stepped back and ducked beneath the big man's grasp and gave the miner a solid blow under the heart. It froze the miner in his tracks. Tuck followed up with a left hook to the temple. Kelly jumped up and down as she yelled, "Hit him again, Tuck!" He glanced in her direction.

When the miner raised his hands to protect his face, Tuck gave him another blow to the heart. The man lowered his arms. Tuck nailed him with a solid right to the nose. Blood spurted from both nostrils.

Tuck landed three more solid blows. The miner wouldn't go down. He just seemed to get madder and madder and kept charging. Tuck feinted and smashed a left to the miner's ribs. He feinted again and started to swing. The miner lunged with both fists flailing. A roundhouse left staggered Tuck causing him to trip over a crate and fall off the porch.

"Leave him alone, you drunken bum!" Kelly yelled. She looked around trying to find someone to stop the fight.

The miner hurled himself through the air, landed on Tuck's chest so hard it knocked the wind out of him, and pinned him to the hard, caked dirt. Tuck turned and twisted, but the miner's bulk kept Tuck on his back. When Tuck finally managed to jerk one hand free, he smashed a right to the miner's jaw.

Apparently unaffected by the blow, and with sweat running down his face, the miner wrapped his large hands around Tuck's throat and said, "Now I'm going to kill you."

Kelly grabbed a pick handle out of the box and circled around to the back of the miner. Tuck's face was turning blue. Kelly raised the pick handle and with all the force she could muster landed the heavy wooden handle square in the middle of the miner's skull. The blow sounded like a ripe melon hitting the floor. The big man's eyes sunk back in his head and he stopped moving. Tuck gasped to catch his breath. Then with a shove he rolled the unconscious man off him.

Kelly bent over and helped drag Tuck to his feet. "Come on," she said. "Let's get out of here before he wakes up."

Tuck rubbed his neck and said, "He looks as if he's out for a while. But you're right, we'd better get a move on." He hoisted the bundle of supplies to his shoulder and headed west. Kelly followed close behind.

When they came to a small stream, Tuck stopped and said, "This must be Annie Creek. The storekeeper said it will lead us down into Spearfish Canyon."

"I sure hope so," said Kelly. "I don't think I've ever been so tired and my feet are burning like fire."

They followed the creek for about a half hour before Kelly started limping badly and falling behind. Tuck stopped and waited for her. When she caught up, she said, "I'm sorry, Tuck. Can't we rest for a minute?"

Tuck put the bundle of supplies on the ground and said, "We've gone far enough for now. Besides, I doubt anybody cares enough about that drunken miner to follow us and he's in no shape to do it." He chuckled, then said, "That was some wallop you gave him. It's a good thing too. He had both my arms pinned and I was ready to pass out. I was completely helpless. I tried to get my gun out, but it was no use."

She looked into his eyes and smiled. "After all you've done for me, it's the least I could do. But why did he act like he knew you, like he was out to get you?"

Tuck rubbed his neck again. "Remember when I told you I'd helped Ira out of a jam? Well, that miner was one of the gang picking on him. Guess he didn't like the fact I got the better of them."

Kelly was surprised, but pleased, when Tuck leaned down, put one arm around her back, the other under her knees, and lifted her off her feet. Being in his arms made her feel warm and cozy. She completely forgot about her hurting feet. He carried her down to the creek's edge and placed her on the moss-covered bank. In her whole life, no man had ever treated her so gently.

"Soak your feet in the cold water," Tuck said. "I'll get out the medicine I brought." He climbed back up to the road and started to retrieve the bundle of supplies. Before picking them up, he gazed intently at the surrounding landscape.

"Do you see something?" she yelled up to him.

He quickly picked up the package, returned to her side, and said, "I don't like the looks of those clouds rolling in. I think, if we can find some shelter, we should camp here for the night." He patted her on top of her rust-colored hair, and said, "You keep soaking your feet. I want to take a closer look at those rocks over there."

Kelly's gaze followed Tuck as he crossed the stream and fought his way through a mass of fallen timber and tangled brush. Once he cleared the obstacles, it took only a couple of minutes before he reached the rocks and disappeared from sight. When he reappeared, he was smiling.

After working his way back, he said, "We're in luck. Mother Nature and someone else, probably a miner panning the stream, has left us a perfect spot to spend the night. But first, we'll doctor your feet. Then we'll go up, make camp, and fix something to eat."

He took his neckerchief from around his neck and handed it to Kelly. "Dry your feet with this. I'll get the medicine ready."

Tuck gently applied the salve to her raw blisters. His touch gave her a strange contented feeling. When he finished applying the salve, he neatly wrapped her feet with bandages and helped her put on the heavy wool socks. If he only knew what she was thinking, he'd probably run away. She slipped into her shoes and with Tuck's help stood up and said, "They feel much better now. Let's go fix something to eat, I'm still starved."

Kelly followed Tuck up the slope and into the shelter. After looking around, she understood what Tuck meant about Mother Nature and a miner. The exterior of the shelter consisted of three huge flat slabs of rock. Two vertical side rocks, starting about twelve feet apart, extended several feet out from the surface of the slope and gently angled inward. The rock on the left was about two feet higher and longer than the one on the right. The space between them left a narrow mazelike doorway. The third slab rested horizontally across the other two with an overhang extending a few inches on each side and above the entrance. Someone had dug out the inside, leaving a triangle-shaped room with a dirt flat floor and a straight backwall. A circle of stones lay two or three feet inside the door. The stone above the circle was blackened with a smoke trail leading to a six-inch crack between the top of the left wall and roof.

Tuck smiled and said, "Think this place with keep us dry for tonight?"

"This little cave is perfect," she said. "Maybe we can make it our new home?"

Tuck answered with, "Why don't you go out and gather some wood for the fire? I'll cut some spruce boughs for our beds."

By the time Tuck finished cutting and laying out the boughs, Kelly had amassed a stack of dry firewood. He quickly started a small fire in the circle of stones and in a few minutes the smell of sizzling bacon, steaming beans, and boiling coffee permeated their little shelter. Kelly's mouth watered. Hunger pangs rolled in her stomach.

After a meal as good as any she'd ever tasted, they leaned against the right rock wall to finish their coffee. Outside, rolling black clouds churned the sky. A strong wind came up, dropping the temperature. Inside, the fire's heat reflecting off the rocks made their accommodations warm and pleasant. She smiled at Tuck and said, "This is the first time since I got off the stage that I feel safe. Can't we just stay here? Maybe we can find enough gold to buy what we need. It won't be much."

Tuck poured them another cup of coffee. He stared at the fire for a while, then said, "We can't stay here. I've got a job to do and I've already been away too long. George Hearst might be needing me right now."

After they finished their coffee and wiped their dishes clean, Tuck reached into the bundle of supplies and brought out the two peppermint sticks. Kelly clapped her hands and said, "Oh, Tuck. You think of everything."

With a slight blush to his cheeks, he said, "I've always had a taste for peppermint candy. When I saw them in the store, I just couldn't resist buying us some."

A teeth-jarring crack of thunder followed by a flash of night-splitting lightning broke the mood. Within seconds a torrential rain turned the outside into a wall of water. Not a drop found its way inside.

Tuck went back to the package and removed two blankets. He handed one to her and said, "Might as well get some sleep. We'll get an early start in the morning." He built up the fire for the night, rolled himself a cigarette, and lit it with a burning twig. Then he leaned back against the wall again and blew his smoke into the air.

Suddenly Kelly asked, "Tuck, do you have a wife?"

The question brought him up straight as he said, "Not anymore, I don't."

Kelly eased over and sat beside Tuck. "What happened to her?" she asked.

"What happened to her?" he repeated. "I guess you'd have to say I killed her."

Kelly gasped. "I don't believe that for a minute."

Tuck took another drag of his cigarette, then tossed the butt into the fire. "Her name was Mary Lou and we were married less than a year. I loved her very much and worried about her safety. Because my job kept me away for days at a time, I thought it would be a good idea for her to have a dog. She really didn't want one but I insisted." He took a deep breath and wiped a tear from his eye.

Kelly's heart was breaking from the hurt she heard in his voice. She patted him gently on the arm. "That was very thoughtful," she said.

"Yes. I thought I was doing the right thing. But I was wrong."

Kelly was almost afraid to go on, but finally she said, "Why? What happened?"

Tuck poured himself the last cup of coffee, took a deep gulp, and then went on with his story. "It was a Saturday afternoon and I was out of town on a case. Evidently the dog wanted to go out, so she took him for a walk in the park. From what the police told me, she was attacked and killed by a gang of Barbary Coast thugs."

Kelly fought to hold back tears as she said, "But you didn't kill her."

Tuck shook his head. "I feel that I did. At least I'm responsible for her death. She didn't want that dog. If I hadn't insisted, she'd still be alive."

Kelly took Tuck's hand in hers, looked him in the eye, and said, "What happened to Mary Lou was fate. Even if she didn't have the dog, she could have been walking in the park, or a carriage could have hit her. The only people responsible for her death are her attackers. You must stop blaming yourself."

How she wanted to wrap her arms around him and make the hurt go away. She was sorry she had brought up the subject. She moved to the other side of the fire, stretched out on her makeshift bed, and pulled the blanket over her. "Good night, Tuck," she said. "Tomorrow will be a better day."

Through mostly closed eyes, she watched as Tuck put a stick of wood on the fire then lay down with his back toward her. In a few minutes, she heard his slow steady breathing.

Chapter Nine

Tuck woke just as dawn was breaking. The aftereffects of the fight with the miner had his body aching from eyelash to toenail, even more than the day before. That big miner hadn't missed a spot. When he was sure all his parts were still working, he rolled out and struggled to a standing position. He then grabbed the coffeepot and went outside.

The rain had stopped and the sky was cloudless. Tuck stretched his aching arms, first out from his sides and then over his head, hoping to loosen his tight muscles. He did a couple of knee bends and then went down to the stream and threw water on his face. The cold water did the trick. He ran his fingers through his blond hair, filled the pot, and went back to the cave. By the time the coffee and bacon was ready, Kelly was awake and sitting upright on her bedroll.

"If that bacon tastes as good as it smells, you're going to have a hard time talking me into leaving here," she said through a bright smile. "And if I don't leave you can't either because you already said you'd take care of me."

Tuck knew she was teasing and he liked the way she

was looking at him, but he did feel a bit uncomfortable. "Breakfast's almost ready," Tuck said. "Better get up now and do what you have to do. We'll eat as soon as you're ready and then get an early start."

Kelly bit her lip and with a cute little pout said, "Do we really have to leave? I like being here alone with you."

"We went through this yesterday, Kelly. We agreed that I was going to take you to Ira's cabin and leave you there while I go back to work. I'm sure it won't be for long and I know you're going to like Ira."

Her pout changed to a smile as she said, "I feel as if I could walk a hundred miles this morning. You really fixed my blisters. Maybe you should be a doctor."

Tuck was amazed how a little flattering from this young woman could make him feel like a teenager. "Oh, I didn't do anything except put a little salve on them. It must've been the good night's rest that did it." He handed her a plate of food and said, "Eat this so we can break camp and get on our way."

Tuck piled three slices of bacon on a hunk of bread for himself, then doubled the edges over the sizzling meat. It was delicious. He glanced over at Kelly and noticed she seemed to be enjoying her food as much as he was.

Soon as they finished eating, Tuck divided their supplies into two piles: one big, one small. He wrapped a blanket around each pile and handed the smaller one to Kelly. "Time to head out."

Outside, Kelly paused and patted one of the rocks forming the doorway and said, "Good-bye, little cave, you've been a good home."

Tuck smiled. How different she sounded. All elements of fright seemed to have evaporated from her tone.

The journey down Annie Creek turned out to be a nightmare. The gully carved by the running water was wall-to-wall brush and downfall. What open space there was was overgrown with dark-green nettles that the smallest touch made your skin feel as if it was on fire. Then the gully turned into a descent so steep the only way to proceed was to sit down and slide. At the bottom, they broke through the underbrush and found themselves on the floor of a huge canyon.

Kelly rushed into the open, spun around a few times, and said, "Oh, Tuck. I've never seen such a beautiful place."

"Me neither," said Tuck.

The canyon looked to be about a half-mile wide. A large stream raised mist and bubbles as it raced down the center. A wagon road had been built alongside the stream. Pink, yellow, red, and purple flowers covered the open space between the water and the edges of the canyon. But it was the canyon's walls that took their breath away.

One side of the canyon was made up of towering formations of flat gray rocks decorated with streaks of red. The rocks were stacked one upon another with such mechanical regularity they seemed to have been placed by the hand of a master stonemason. On the other side, the walls were covered with majestic pines like stately sentinels guarding the valley below.

Tuck set his bundle on the ground and took out Ira's map. "Looks like we have to go upstream until we hit a string of beaver dams. At the third dam we follow a trail through the woods to the cabin."

"How long will it take?" asked Kelly, peering up into Tuck's eyes.

"No way of telling," Tuck said. "I would guess that if we hurry we should be there before dark. We'll make better time by sticking to the road, but if we hear someone coming we've got to take cover."

Kelly gave him a quizzical look and asked, "Why? They won't know who we are and maybe they'll give us a ride."

"We can't chance it, Kelly. By now both the sheriff and Charley Utter are out to get you. It's only been three days and there might even be a reward. It would be easy for someone to put two and two together. That fight yesterday was bad enough. We don't need anything else to draw at-

tention to us." He picked up his blanket roll and started up
the road.

After an hour of steady walking, Tuck heard a faint
pounding. He motioned for Kelly to be silent. Cupping his
hand behind his ear, he listened intently. "Horses," he said,
"running at a fast clip downstream in our direction." He
took Kelly's hand. "We've got to get out of sight."

Side by side they ran toward a stand of quaking ash and
hid in the underbrush. Within seconds, three men, pushing
their mounts to their fullest, came bounding down the road.
Tuck went for his gun. "Those are the guys that held up
the stage," he whispered.

Kelly grabbed his hand. "Let them go, Tuck. There's too
many of them. You can tell the sheriff when you get back
to town."

"You're right," he said as he returned his Colt to his belt
and watched the robbers disappear around a bend. "Let's
get going."

When the sun was directly overhead, they stopped and
shared a can of peaches and the bacon left over from breakfast.

With the peaches gone, Kelly raised the can to her mouth
and swallowed the last of the sweet juice. "Tuck, are you
sure I'll be safe with this man Ira? Can't you at least stay
for a few days to see if I like it there?"

Tuck clenched his teeth and shook his head as he said,
"Kelly, I want to do everything I can to make you feel safe,
but you know I've got a job to do. I've taken good care of
you so far, haven't I? If I wasn't sure of Ira, I wouldn't be
taking you there." He reached out and put his hand on her
shoulder. "It's important that you trust me and try to make
the best out of what we are doing. I've already said that
I'll help you get back to San Francisco as soon as I can.
But you've got to be patient."

When she looked as if she wanted to cry, Tuck sighed
and was sorry he spoke so sternly to her. Truth was, he
really didn't know much about Ira except that he appeared

to be well educated. Sure, he'd taken an immediate liking to the old gray-haired man, but it was only intuition that made him believe she'd be safe with him. Problem was, he had no other choice.

Tuck gently put his arm around her, gave her a slight squeeze, and said, "If after you meet Ira and you don't want to stay, I'll try to find you another place."

The words were what she was looking for; a smile quickly replaced the frown.

They followed the road for another hour and then came to a fork in the stream. One branch continued straight ahead, the other turned off to the right. "Which way do we go?" Kelly asked.

He took out the map, studied it, and said, "This doesn't show any fork. I'm pretty sure Ira would have put it in if it was important."

"Does that mean we're lost?" Kelly asked with that worried look Tuck had learned to recognize.

He smiled to make her feel better and said, "I don't think so. I just think we're further downstream than the area covered by the map. We'll go straight ahead and hope it doesn't take too long to find those beaver dams."

Sometime later, they rounded a huge stand of white birch trees and saw the canyon stretching ahead. For at least a mile, groves of quaking ash and birch, their leaves flickering and quivering in the light breeze, sheltered the stream. Tuck smiled. That many trees meant there had to be beaver.

In no time they discovered where the beaver had turned the stream into a series of ponds. Each pond had a overflow where foaming water gushed over its face, ran a few feet and then into another dam. For over a mile, the ponds connected to one another like a string of pearls.

At the third dam, a footpath crossed the mass of mud and sticks forming the face and led to a trail leading into the woods. It had to be the path to Ira's cabin. They followed the well-marked trail through a thick forest of pine and spruce. When they finally broke into the open, they were facing a log cabin about thirty feet long. The back of the cabin rested against the base of a mountain. A stone chimney, sending smoke curling into the afternoon air, formed the right end of the cabin. A huge stack of split firewood rested against the left.

Tuck cupped his hands around his mouth and yelled, "Hello the cabin!"

The door opened a crack. Then it swung open and a growling large, gray, wolflike dog burst into the open and headed straight for Tuck and Kelly. Tuck pulled his navy Colt and stepped between Kelly and the charging animal.

As Tuck pulled back the hammer to shoot, Ira came out and shouted, "Down, Armstrong! Get back here!" The dog stopped but his mouth maintained a ferocious show of teeth.

When Ira finally recognized Tuck, he broke into a smile, and dragging his bad leg, hurried to greet them. He gave the snarling dog a light swat across the nose, and said, "Mr. Powells, I'm very sorry for the greeting Armstrong has given you, but we don't have many visitors and he feels he must protect me." He grabbed Tuck's hand and said, "I'm happy you've come to see me." He then looked at Kelly and asked, "And who's this fine-looking young man?"

With a big smile on his face, Tuck said, "Ira, it's good to see you again. But please call me Tuck." He took Kelly by the arm and said, "This here is Kelly." He paused, "I'm afraid this isn't a social visit. We need your help. Can we go inside and talk about it?"

"Why, of course. That's what friends are for. Let's go in and I'll put up a fresh pot of coffee. And I've got some cinnamon rolls I just took out of the oven." He turned on his good leg, led the way to the door, and held it open. Armstrong was last to enter.

Chapter Ten

Kelly stepped inside the cabin and looked around in amazement. She knew Ira lived alone, but instead of being dirty and messy as she had expected, the cabin's interior was beautiful. The log walls surrounding the one long room, divided by function, were so highly varnished she could see her reflection in them.

To her right, a huge stone fireplace highlighted the living room section. In front of the fireplace stood a bent-willow settee covered with a yellow-and-brown afghan. On each side of the settee were bent-willow armchairs facing inward and covered with blue-and-gray Indian blankets. A multi-colored oval rag rug covered the space between the settee and the fireplace. Two end tables, each holding a coal-oil lamp centered on a white linen doily, completed the furnishings for the parlor area.

She did an about-face and saw, standing against the kitchen wall, a majestic cast-iron cook stove. Its warming oven above the cooking surface was decorated with blue-and-white porcelain trimmed in polished steel. The over-sized oven door was adorned with the same material. A coffeepot and huge iron kettle shared the stovetop. The delicious aroma of coffee, cinnamon, and whatever was cooking in the kettle filled the room, reminding her of the way she felt about the bacon they had for breakfast.

A dry sink and work counter stood to the left of the stove. Both under and over the counter were open shelves crowded with cans, mason jars, and bottles. On the right end of the sink was a water bucket with a dipper hanging by its handle. A bin full of split firewood was to the right of the stove. Kelly couldn't get over how clean and orderly everything was. She smiled at the old man and said, "You've got a nice place, Ira."

He returned her smile, looking a little embarrassed by the compliment.

The dining area consisted of a table and four straight-backed chairs occupying the area between the stove and the back of the settee. A red-and-white checked cloth covered the table. In the center stood a milk-white vase full of purple wildflowers.

Kelly's anxiety had calmed to the point where she no longer feared staying there with Ira. Two bunks, one on each side of a door in the rear wall, were anchored to the logs so that only front legs were needed for support. Red-and-black Indian blankets covered the mattresses. Then it hit her. Where would she sleep? The bunks couldn't be moved to give her privacy. She turned to look at Tuck and saw that the two men were still standing in the open doorway. "Aren't you gentlemen coming in?" she asked.

Ira closed the door and said, "You folks have a seat in front of the fireplace while I put up some fresh coffee." He limped to the sink, emptied the old grounds in a bucket, and used the dipper to fill the pot. "Hope you folks like it strong," he said as he poured in ground coffee. Then he wiped his hands on a cloth draped over his shoulder and sat down in the chair opposite Tuck. "Now, what is it you want to talk about?"

Kelly waited till both men were seated before easing herself onto the settee. Armstrong strolled over and stretched out at her feet. She reached down and patted his head while she listened to Tuck explain why there were there.

When Tuck finished, Ira leaned close enough to Kelly for her to see tiny red veins running through the oversized white sections surrounding his dark-brown irises. "Don't you worry, little missy," he said. "Old Ira and Armstrong'll make sure nobody else hurts you. But now I'd better get to that pot before it boils over."

Ira limped to the stove, grabbed the pot's handle with the cloth, and slid it off the hot cooking surface. He removed the lid with his left hand and used a large spoon in his right hand to stir the contents. A cloud of steam filled the air above the stove.

Kelly got up and said, "What is that you're cooking? It smells delicious."

"Dried codfish stew," said Ira. "It's one of George Hearst's favorite meals. But he likes me to make it the day before he comes to visit. He says it's better if it stands overnight."

Tuck hurried to Ira and asked, "Are you saying that George Hearst will be here tomorrow?"

"Yep," said Ira. "This cabin really belongs to him. When he gets fed up with all the fighting and problems in Lead City, he gets up early and without telling anyone where he's going, hikes out here and spends a day or two."

"I'll be darned," said Tuck. "How'd you meet him?"

Ira scratched his head with the spoon handle as he said, "Well, it happened this way." He put down the spoon and went on. "For years I lived in my little cave here." He used a match to light one of the lamps, then limped across the room to the door between the two bunks. He opened the door and led them into a room built into the side of the mountain. It was sparsely furnished with a double-decked bunk, a small stove, and a dropdown table attached to the heavy timbers supporting the overhead rocks. The room was a little damp, but clean. Of course it couldn't hold a candle to the cabin.

Kelly grinned, grabbed Ira's free hand, and asked, "Can I use this room? I'll be out of your way in here."

Ira set the lamp on the table, returned her smile, nodded, and said, "I was going to sleep in here and let you have a bunk in the cabin, but if you like it in here, it's yours. I just want you to know you won't be a bother wherever you sleep."

"Thank you, Ira," said Kelly as she pictured how she was going to fix up the room.

When they returned to their seats in the main cabin, Tuck said to Ira, "You were telling me how you know George Hearst?"

"I was, wasn't I," said Ira. "Like I said, I lived for several years in that little cave back there. One day while I was splitting firewood I looked up and saw a big man with a long gray beard walking up the trail." Ira rubbed his leg. "He introduced himself as Hearst. Then just as if he'd known me for years, he took the axe out of my hand and started chopping. 'Take a break,' he said. After splitting several chunks, he stopped, leaned on the axe handle, and said, 'Sure could use a cool drink of water.' "

Ira, as if he was purposely stretching out his story, went to the stove and stirred the pot again. He then filled three cups of coffee and asked, "You folks want to take your coffee here at the table or over there where it's more comfortable? We're going to try out those cinnamon rolls I told you about."

After taking seats at the table and each having a warm roll, Ira went on with his story. "George and me seemed to hit it off right away. He told me how, when he was a boy, he used to work alongside his father's slaves and how, when his father died, he freed them. And how he went to California to hunt for gold and how he eventually wound up in the Black Hills. Then he wanted to know about my life, so I told him. We must've talked for hours."

"Please go on," said Kelly.

"Well, it started getting late," said Ira. "So I invited him to stay for supper and spend the night. I had a pot of pig's feet and sauerkraut on the stove. When he saw that he went crazy. Seems it was a favorite of his. Man, can he eat. He ate a whole loaf of fresh-baked bread. Oh-oh, that reminds me." Ira went to the stove and removed two loaves of un-baked bread he had rising in the warming oven. After brushing the tops with melted butter, he slid them into the oven. "Need a good hot fire for bread," he said as he stuck the poker inside the firebox and riled up the coals. After putting in three sticks of fresh wood, Ira came back and sat in his chair.

"To make a long story short," Ira said. "George stayed for two days. Then he started coming out every couple of weeks." The room was filling with the aroma of baking bread. "One day he showed up with a bunch of men and they built this cabin. Only took them two days. The fol-lowing week a dray showed up with this stove and the furniture. After that, George just sort of took over. But I've got to tell you, I couldn't have found a better friend."

Suddenly what Ira was saying sunk in. He didn't own the cabin. Kelly felt a pang of anxiety as she asked, "What if Mr. Hearst doesn't want me to stay here?"

"Don't you worry about that," said Ira. "When he hears your story, I'm sure he'll want to help."

"I sure hope so," said Kelly.

Tuck turned to Ira and said, "Ira, I've just got to ask you something. Why were you dressed like you were and why did you talk like you did when I first met you?"

Before answering, Ira closed his eyes and rested his chin on his chest for a second. "Men in these parts don't cotton to uppity black folks. When I go to town I dress and act like they expect me to. Most of the time they leave me alone. That bunch you drove off were a lot meaner than most of them."

Kelly never felt so sorry for anyone in her life. "That's awful," she said.

"You get used to it," said Ira. "But don't you worry about me. You've got enough problems of your own."

Tuck stared at Ira and said, "Would you mind telling us what your real background is?"

Ira thought for a second, then said, "While I fix us some supper, I'll consider it. I'm thinking of frying up some venison steaks, okay? I've got to save the fish stew for tomorrow."

Tuck said, "Sounds good to me. How about you, Kelly?"

"I'm so hungry I could eat a whole deer," said Kelly. "Can I help?"

"Well, you can peel some potatoes," said Ira. He turned to Tuck and said, "If you wouldn't mind, we could use a fresh bucket of water. The spring is in that little draw off to our right. While you're down there, bring us each a bottle of malt beer, and Kelly a bottle of root beer. You'll find them in a little ice-cave next to the spring. And bring that haunch of venison so I can cut us some steaks."

Tuck picked up the water bucket and was on his way out the door when Ira threw him a clean flour sack and said, "You can put the beer and venison in this."

After a delicious supper, Kelly washed and dried the dishes. Ira swept the floor and Tuck went outside to fetch a load of firewood.

As Kelly was putting the last dish away, she looked at Ira and said, "You sure are a good cook. And I really want you to know how grateful I am for you letting me stay here. So many things have happened to me since I got off that stage, I don't know if I'm coming or going."

Before Ira could answer, Tuck came in with his arms full of wood. He used the toe of his boot to lift the lid of the woodbin. He dropped the wood inside and said, "It's getting cold out there."

Ira stood up and said, "I think maybe I should start a fire in Kelly's room."

When Ira came out from starting the fire, Kelly said, "I'd love to hear how you learned to cook. Cooking was never my cup of tea; maybe you can give me some pointers."

"First let me light the fireplace," said Ira. "Then we'll take our seats in front of the fire and I'll tell you a little bit about old Ira." He chuckled for a second and said with a big grin, "I'll even try not to lie too much."

Kelly dropped down on the rug next to Armstrong while Tuck and Ira went back to their armchairs. Ira crossed his arms, looked down at Kelly, and said, "I was born in New York City. My mother and father were domestics for the Astor family. But my parents were proud people and wanted something better for me. After I finished elementary school, I was accepted at Avery College; at the time it was a new school for black folks. I decided to study to be a teacher." He paused for a moment. "While I was in college, I got me a job in the kitchen so I could earn a little spending money. Funny thing was, I discovered I liked working in the kitchen better than I did my schoolwork. But I didn't want to let my folks down, so I studied hard and graduated."

"And that's how you learned to cook?" asked Kelly.

"Not quite," said Ira. "When I returned to New York, I didn't even look for a teaching job. I went to the Delmonico Hotel and signed on as an apprentice chef. I was still working there when the war broke out. One of our best customers was an army officer named Sherman. When President Lincoln made him a general, he enlisted me in the army and had me assigned to his personal staff. After the war, the general went out west to fight the Indians and took me with him."

Ira's leg must have started hurting. He rubbed it a couple times before getting up and pacing slowly around the room. "On Sherman's staff was a Colonel Custer. The colonel took a liking to me and pestered the general until he assigned me as his personal cook. I was with Custer when he led his expedition into the Black Hills. Tuck can tell you what happened after that. Right now I've got to go get some whiskey for this pain."

Kelly patted the dog's head and said, "So you're named after General Custer?" She looked up at Tuck. "I won't be afraid to stay with Ira. Outside of you, I think he's the nicest man I've ever met." His sudden blush amused her.

Tuck had just finished telling her about Ira's discharge from the army when Ira came back inside. It had been a long day and the heat and dancing fire was making it hard for her to hold her eyes open. She yawned, stretched her arms, and asked, "Would you gentlemen mind if I turned in?"

Both men stood up. Tuck said, "I'm ready to hit the sack myself."

Minutes later, after blowing out the lamp and crawling into her bunk, she thought about Tuck and Ira and how they were quickly changing her outlook on life. And on men.

Chapter Eleven

Tuck laughed to himself watching the two old friends bantering with each other. It had started as soon as George Hearst came through the cabin door and had been going strong ever since. Hearst pulled out a plug of Horseshoe and started to bite off a chew. Ira put his hand on Hearst's arm and said, "Now, George. You know I don't appreciate tobacco chewing in the cabin."

Hearst stuffed the tobacco plug back into his pocket. It was amazing how this mining tycoon, who could buy or sell almost anyone or anything, responded to the admonition of his skinny old friend.

Hearst smiled and said, "Ira, you're worse than my wife, Phoebe. If it wasn't for your cooking, I'd be better off staying in town."

Ira turned to Tuck and Kelly. "I've never met the lady, but from what I hear, this bullheaded old codger has a beautiful wife. But instead of staying home with her and their son and maybe spending some of the money he's got stashed away, he insists on tramping around the mountains looking for gold. I'll bet if he lives to be five hundred, he'll still be sitting in some mining camp trying to beat an old prospector out of his claim."

Hearst tried to look angry as he shook his fist at Ira and said, "Don't you be telling these young folks bad things about me. You may think I've got a lot of money and I probably have more than I deserve but I've got a feeling that when I'm gone, my son Willie will run through it in a hurry. He's got Phoebe wrapped around his little finger. I'm afraid she'll let him do whatever he wants." He filled a coffee cup, carried it to the table, and took a seat. He took a long swig and put down his cup before he leaned back in his chair and hooked his thumbs behind the bib of his overalls. "Tuck," he said, "why don't you tell me how it is that you and this young lady happen to be in the company of this old belly-robber?"

After Tuck and Kelly each gave their versions of the past three days, Hearst reached out, took Kelly's hand, and said, "From what you tell me, I don't think any jury in the world will convict you of murder. But we can't take any chances."

He turned to Tuck. "When you get back to town, I want you to spend some time at Charley Utter's place. See what you can find out about that night. Talk to that girl, Trixie. Maybe she'll know what Utter has up his sleeve."

Hearst released Kelly's hand and said, "We're going to get you out of this. It's the least I can do. Jack Phillips told me that the man you killed in Charley Utter's place was hired to get me out of the way. So you see, I may owe you my life."

"Anything else you want from me?" Tuck asked.

Hearst used the fingers of his right hand to comb his long beard. "Well, if you got time, try to get a line on anything else Archie Bowlan has planned. There's nothing I like better than a good fight, but I like to know what I'm fighting." He stopped combing and reached into his pocket. "One more thing," he said as he handed Tuck two twenty-dollar gold pieces. "Take this money and buy Kelly some proper clothes. When I get back to town, I'll find a way to get them out here to her."

Tuck stuffed the money into his watch pocket and asked, "When will you be back in town?"

"Well," he said, "that depends." He winked at Kelly. "If Ira don't kick me out sooner, I'll leave here day after to-morrow."

Tuck shook hands all around and headed for the door. Before he got outside, Kelly ran to him, grabbed his arm, and said, "Please be careful; don't take any chances."

"I won't," Tuck said as he stared into her eyes and resisted the urge to take her in his arms. Then he quickly went out the door and headed down the path. Before entering the forest, he turned and looked back at Kelly standing in the open door. She waved one more time, then went inside, leaving an emptiness in Tuck's heart.

Tuck leaned against Charley Utter's long polished bar and surveyed the crowded room. A dozen or more skimpily clad women slithered from table to table. Some were serving drinks; others were hustling the men to buy drinks for them. As long as someone was willing to pay, they downed one drink after another. Tuck wondered how they managed to stay sober.

Several girls tried to get him to buy them a drink, but none of them sounded or looked like the one he was looking for. Then he saw a tall girl coming down the stairs. She fit the description of Trixie that Kelly had given him. He rushed across the room, met her at the foot of the stairs, and said, "Is your name Trixie?"

She gave him a smile that made him think she'd known him for life and said, "It sure is, cowboy. You going to buy me a drink or maybe you'd rather visit my room?"

Tuck pondered the choices for a second and then said, "I'd be pleased to buy you a drink."

She quickly hooked her arm in his, led him to a vacant table, and motioned to one of the other girls. When the waiter girl came up to the table, Trixie said, "Bring me my usual." She turned to Tuck. "What's your pleasure, cowboy?"

"Just bring me a mug of beer," said Tuck.

Tuck watched till the waiter girl was out of hearing range, then he turned back to Trixie and said, "My name is Tuck Powells. I'm a friend of Kelly Ryan and she needs your help."

Trixie's eyes, now the size of silver dollars, were filled with curiosity. "Did she get away? I've been worried sick about her. You must make sure she's careful. The sheriff is looking for her, but even worse—if Charley Utter gets her before the sheriff, she'll pay a horrible price for killing that guy." She paused for a second. "She is the one who killed him, isn't she?"

Before Tuck had a chance to answer, the waiter girl was back with the drinks. Trixie downed hers and ordered another. This time when the girl walked away, Trixie said, "You've got to keep buying me drinks or I can't sit here."

Tuck took a sip of beer then said, "This is crazy. Can't we go someplace and talk?"

Trixie looked around to see if anyone was listening. "We can go up to my room, but you'll have to pay."

Tuck looked at Trixie but his thoughts were on Kelly. "No thanks," he said. "I'll just keep the drinks coming. But how can you hold so much whiskey?"

"We girls don't drink whiskey. We drink tea and you guys pay for whiskey."

Tuck had heard that the girls on the coast were forced to do that, but somehow it never dawned on him that they would be doing the some thing in the Black Hills. Trixie was downing her third drink and Tuck hadn't learned a thing. He was about to ask what they were saying about the one-eyed man's murder when a tall, heavy-chested man dressed in black broadcloth and wearing a wide-brimmed hat with a flat crown pulled out the chair next to Trixie and sat down. Ignoring Tuck, he grabbed her hand and said,

"I've been looking for you. Let's go upstairs and whoop it up."

Trixie pulled her hand away and said, "Frank! Can't you see I'm busy now? Stick around; soon as I'm finished with this customer, you can have your fun."

The man tensed and a frown curled his lips as he said, "What's the matter, my money ain't good enough for you? You always told me I was your favorite customer. Now's the time to prove it. You get up out of that chair and go upstairs. I'll be right behind you." He shook his finger at Tuck and growled, "You hear what I say, cowboy. This is my woman, so you just go find another one."

Tuck rose slowly to his feet and said, "Why don't you be a nice guy and wait your turn. She's busy now."

Tuck's words brought the man leaping to his feet so hard it sent his chair flying behind him. With clenched fists and set feet Frank said, "I've heard enough from you, cowboy. Now you're going to be history!"

Without a hint of urgency or nervousness, Tuck swung and landed a right to Frank's jaw, sending him staggering back. Before he could recover, Frank was looking down the barrel of Tuck's navy Colt. Frank froze in his tracks with a stunned expression on his face.

Out of the corner of his eye, Tuck saw several men rushing in his direction. Could he handle all of them? he wondered. He moved just enough to keep his Colt trained on Frank while at the same time covering the approaching men. "Don't do anything you'll be sorry for," Tuck said.

The man leading the group was short with long hair. He too was dressed in black with a long chain of gold coins stretching from one vest pocket to the other. Trixie jumped up, blocked the man's way, and said, "Charley! My friend and I were just going upstairs when Frank started making trouble. I explained to him that he was next in line, but he wouldn't listen."

Charley Utter looked Tuck up and down and said, "Kind of quick on the draw, aren't ya?"

Tuck gave Charley the same type of go-over. So this was the man who hurt Kelly. It took all the control he could muster to keep from turning the Colt on him and making him pay for what he had done. But this was not the time or place. He stuffed the Colt back into his belt and said, "The lady and I were discussing business." He nodded toward Frank. "This guy butted in." He took Trixie by the arm and said, "Shall we go upstairs now?"

They were halfway up the stairs when Charley, leaning against the bottom post of the hand carved railing, yelled out, "Trixie, hurry up and give that cowboy what he wants, then get back down here. Frank will be waiting at the bar."

Tuck slowed to a stop and considered going back down to give the little loudmouthed varmint his due for hurting Kelly. But he had a job to do and it wouldn't be too smart to risk losing his temper. They picked up the pace and hurried into Trixie's room. "Is this room like the one Kelly had?" he asked.

"Yes," she said. "All the rooms are basically the same; some of the furniture is more beat up than others." She closed the door, moved chest to chest with Tuck, and stared him in the eye. "What do you want to do?"

He took a deep breath and said, "I just want to talk to you about Kelly and what happened that night."

Trixie looked confused, like she was experiencing something that had never happened to her before. Finally she sat on the bed, clasped her hands in her lap, and said, "But like I told you, you still have to pay me or I'll get into trouble."

Tuck, feeling a bit uncomfortable, wondered what Mary Lou would have thought. But Mary Lou was gone and he couldn't do anything about that. But maybe he could still help Kelly and nothing else really mattered. "Don't worry about it," he said. "I'll pay you the same as anyone else. But now tell me about Kelly."

It only took a few minutes for Trixie to tell all she knew, which wasn't much more than Kelly had already told him.

When she said she had watched Charley hit Kelly and push her inside his office, Tuck asked, "Will you testify to that in court?"

Beads of sweat appeared on her brow. She went to the water pitcher and poured herself a drink. "Believe me, I know I should. But if I do, my life won't be worth any more than Kelly's." She took another swallow. "They're saying that besides killing him, Kelly took his money. Do you know if that's true or not?"

Tuck shook his head in disgust. "Kelly didn't take anything except the clothes on her back. And they were almost torn to shreds."

Trixie tightened her lips. "That's what we all thought. The other girls and I think Charley took the money and blamed it on Kelly."

"Did anyone else see Charley hit Kelly?"

"If I had to bet, I'd say the bartender saw everything. But you'll never get anything out of him. There might be some others, but I wouldn't know who they are."

Tuck placed a wooden chair in front of Trixie, sat down, stared into her eyes, and said, "Trixie, Kelly needs your help. If we give you protection before the trial and then enough money to get out of town for a new start, will you tell what you know?"

She didn't answer.

"Well, would you?"

Tears ran down her cheeks.

"Trixie, you've got to help us. It's the only way we can stop Charley Utter from abusing other women. And you know he must be stopped."

She wiped her eyes. "I want to help. I really do, and I want to believe you can protect me, but if you knew Charley like I do . . ."

This was a lot harder than he thought it would be. "Trixie, I'm a detective and I've got Kelly in a safe place. If necessary, I'll put you up with her before the trial."

She let out a sigh and gave a slight nod of her head. "All right, I will. Tell me what you want me to do."

Tuck felt as if he'd won a major battle. "Just go on like nothing's happened. I'll be back in a couple of days and we'll come to your room again and I'll let you know how we are going to handle everything. In the meantime, don't worry about a thing."

Tuck was about to leave when she said, "You've got to give me three dollars."

He gave her a five-dollar gold piece and left the room. At the foot of the stairs stood a fat man in a checkered vest. He looked up at Tuck and said, "Excuse me, sir. My name is Pat Flavin." He stuck out his hand. "I wonder if I could have a word with you?"

Tuck paused for a second, shook his hand, then said, "I don't have much time, but I think I could go for a beer."

The fat man led them to an empty table where they sat down and Pat Flavin ordered two beers and six hard-boiled eggs. He patted his huge stomach and said, "My friend is nearly empty. When he's like that, he gives me a hard time."

Tuck stared at the man and thought that he could probably go for a month without eating. "What do you want to talk about?" he asked.

"I wish they'd hurry with them eggs." He smacked his lips, leaned toward Tuck, and said, "I saw the way you took care of that guy giving you a hard time. I think I might be able to use your services." He swung around in his chair to look in the direction the waiter girl had gone. Not seeing her, he swung back and said, "You don't look like a miner, and I don't think you're a gambler or any of the other types around town." He looked over his shoulder again. "I liked the way you pulled that hogleg before the other guy even knew what was going on. It sure was pretty."

Tuck figured it must be his gun the fat man wanted to hire. "What kind of job you got in mind?"

The waiter girl brought the beer and eggs. Flavin peeled and ate three eggs before saying, "Help yourself."

Tuck shook his head and said, "No thanks."

Flavin grabbed the remaining eggs and started peeling. "I sure do like hen's fruit, even though they don't always like me."

Tuck had seen enough. He pushed back his chair and said, "I'll ask you one more time, what kind of job are you talking about?"

"Take it easy, partner. The job is sort of like what you did to that guy a few minutes ago."

"Go on," Tuck said. "I need more than that."

"Well, I represent a group of mine owners. There's an old millionaire who runs a syndicate of San Francisco fat cats that's sticking his nose into my clients' business. If he keeps it up, that gun of yours will come in real handy."

Tuck couldn't believe his luck. Working on the inside he'd get what he needed to finish this job and head back home. He put on his best poker face and fixed his gaze on a chunk of egg peel hung up on Flavin's left vest pocket. "How much does it pay?"

"Fifty bucks a week, plus expenses."

Tuck stood up and stuck out his hand. "Looks like you got yourself a man. What's our first step?"

Flavin shook Tuck's hand and said, "Be at the DeSmet boardinghouse in Central City at seven tomorrow evening. I'll talk it over with my clients. If they agree, which I'm sure they will, you've got the job. In the meantime, stay out of trouble and don't do anything to call attention to yourself." He gulped down the last egg and the rest of his beer, then got up and left.

As he headed back to his own boardinghouse, Tuck wondered if it wasn't a bit too easy. Was he being set up? But he couldn't be. There was no way Flavin could know who he was. Then it dawned on him. When Kelly killed the one-eyed man, it put them in a bind and they had to get someone else in a hurry. That was all right with him; he'd infiltrated other outfits and got away with it and he was sure he could do it again. But now he had to get some clothes for Kelly. Maybe Mrs. Robinson could take care of that.

Chapter Twelve

Tuck felt a chill in the evening air as he rode up Deadwood Gulch toward Central City. The DeSmet boardinghouse was one of the buildings Shorty had pointed out that first day in the area. He had said it was not only a hotel, but also the headquarters of the Father DeSmet Mining Company.

Tuck tethered his rented horse to the hitching rail, climbed the stairs, and went through a pair of stained glass doors. Inside, he was met by a solemn-faced black woman. "My name is Powells," he said. "I'm supposed to meet Mr. Flavin here."

Without a hint of emotion, she gave Tuck a long look then said, "He's in the dining room with Mr. Bowlan and the others." She pointed to a closed door. "You'd best get in there before he eats all the sandwiches." As she turned away, she shook her head and mumbled, "Lordy me, can that man eat."

Tuck moved to the door and knocked.

"Come on in," someone said.

Inside Tuck found Pat Flavin and four other men seated

around a large table covered with a spotless white cloth. What was left of a plate of sandwiches stood in the center. A bottle of bourbon and several glasses surrounded the plate.

Flavin struggled to lift his heavy body to a standing position, and said, "Mr. Powells, I'm glad you could make it." Pat glanced around the table. "This is the fellow I was telling you about. His name is Tuck Powells and I've told him that if you folks agree, he's got the job of helping us keep your mines. He's fully aware that there may come a time when we might need a man who can hold his own with his gun." Flavin rested his puffy hand on Tuck's shoulder. "You all should have seen the way he handled himself at Charley Utter's place. Not only did he make this troublesome hard case back down, but, without batting an eye, he drew down on Charley and two of his men." Flavin pulled out a chair and motioned for Tuck to take a seat. "I've got a real feeling that Mr. Powells will come in handy before this fight is over."

Tuck nodded to the men as he lowered himself onto his chair.

A man of medium height wearing a white linen shirt with an open collar and blue sleeve garters rose to his feet. "Glad to meet you, Tuck. My name is Archie Bowlan and I own the Father DeSmet. What do you think of our headquarters?" Without giving Tuck a chance to answer, he went on, saying, "Guess it's fitting we hire you. Our last guy lost his job at Utter's place and now Pat has found you in the same joint. Hope you fare better than he did." Archie let out a hearty laugh that was soon joined by the others.

That is, except Tuck, who didn't think the words funny enough to laugh. But he did put on a wry grin and pretended he had no idea what Archie was talking about as he said, "I can take care of myself."

After going around the table introducing General Gashwiler, owner of the Caledonia; Bill Lardner, owner of the Mammoth; and Captain Huron, owner of the Old Abe, he

invited Tuck to help himself to the sandwiches and whiskey.

"Thanks, but I already had supper," said Tuck as he
crossed his long legs under the table. He was starting to
feel more comfortable. None of them looked as if they had
any doubts that he was anything other than a hired gun.

Pat Flavin stuffed a sandwich into his mouth ànd washed
it down with a full glass of bourbon. Then, after brushing
some crumbs from his vest, he leaned back in his chair and
rested his arms across his oversized belly before saying, "I
guess you're all waiting to hear what I've found out. It's
like the old saying goes, I've got good news and I've got
bad news." He rubbed is pudgy hands together. "I'll hit
you with the bad news first."

Pat turned to Bill Lardner and said, "This hurts you more
than the others. After doing some checking, I discovered
that Judge Bennett issued a ruling saying that because the
Black Hills were Indian lands till February '77, any claims
filed before that date are null and void."

Lardner scowled and said, "Why haven't I heard of this
before?"

Flavin shrugged. "In the judge's ruling he gave anyone
who filed before that date the chance to file again. But I
checked the records and it looks as if you failed to protect
your patent on the Mammoth." Pat paused and took another
swig of bourbon. "It gets worse. Hearst must have also
checked and now he's filed on your claim. He's in the
process of applying to the court to obtain legal control."
He let his words sink in before saying, "You can fight him,
but it's going to cost you a lot of money, and I'll tell you
right now, you'll lose."

With his hands shaking like a quaking ash leaf, Lardner
jumped to his feet and said, "This is a bunch of hogwash.
I'm not going to let him take my mine."

Flavin waited for Lardner to settle down a bit before
saying, "Sorry, Bill, but he already has. Your only hope is
to get some money out of him. He'll probably pay to keep

it out of court, but don't push him. Just take his offer and run."

Tuck could now see why Ira had such a high opinion of George. The man didn't leave anything to chance.

Lardner, his face blotched with anger, said, "Hearst probably bought Judge Bennett. I'm going to take this all the way to the Supreme Court!"

"Suit yourself, Bill. But you're wasting your time and money." Pat downed another shot and turned to Captain Huron. "You're in just about as bad a shape as Bill. As you know, your claim runs parallel to the Homestake." He paused for a second. "And that means you run the risk of being wiped out by the Apex Law."

"Apex Law?" Huron's face took on a look of curiosity. "What has the Apex Law got to do with me? I didn't break any of these stupid laws. I've got a perfectly legal claim to the Old Abe."

Tuck couldn't help feeling a bit sorry for these two men. Both of them were about to lose their empires and neither of them could do a thing about it.

Flavin filled Huron's glass with bourbon and handed it to him. "Drink this," he said. "The Apex Law was passed by Congress. In a thumbnail it says that when a miner stakes a claim which contains the apex of a vein of ore, he has the right to follow the vein indefinitely."

Huron let his glass drop to the table. "Look here, Pat. Are you trying to tell me that he can cross over into my claim?"

The fat lawyer nodded and shrugged his shoulders. "That's exactly what it means. And not only the bordering claim, he can keep going till the vein pinches out."

Huron looked like he'd been hit with a hammer. He turned to the others and asked, "Any of you guys heard of this law?"

Lardner said, "Yeah, I heard of it, but like most mine owners I never figured on going deep enough for it to apply to me or any of you others."

Huron took a deep breath, plopped into his chair, and said, "It looks as if Hearst has got me where it hurts. I've suspected for quite some time that the Homestake lode runs through my claim." He laughed sarcastically. "And I thought I was the one putting something over on Hearst. If this law works like you say it does, I might as well hand the Old Abe over to him."

Pat Flavin showed Huron the palm of his hand and said, "Hold your horses, Captain. It's true that Hearst has the vein in his favor, but he needs more than that. It takes surface space to build mills, hoists, carpenter and machine shops. I think we can get you a pretty good price for your claim."

Huron, with a look of total dejection, said, "I hope you're right. I'll wait for him to make me an offer and at least try to get my money back."

Tuck was impressed with Pat Flavin. He might look and act like a fool, but he knew his law. These owners could've done worse in choosing a lawyer.

He was even more impressed when Flavin said, "Captain, if Hearst or one of his people makes you an offer, send them to me. I'll run the price up as high as I can. Of course I'll get ten percent of the sale, but it'll be Hearst paying my commission."

Tuck made a mental note to tell George how they were planning to operate. Pat Flavin couldn't be taken lightly. Too bad he was on the wrong side.

Flavin took a break to devour another sandwich before saying, "Now as far as the DeSmet and Caledonia are concerned, they're pretty safe. But there's no doubt that Hearst wants to get is hands on them too."

General Gashwiler slapped the table with both hands and said, "I still think we ought to put the old polecat out of his misery. Once he gets rolling there's no stopping him. If he can't buy what he wants, or steal what he wants, he'll pay off some judge to give it to him."

Flavin fixed the general with a stern stare. "I know how

you feel, but killing will get us nowhere. Our best bet is to use public opinion. I've got an idea how to make the whole durn Homestake hierarchy look so bad that no public officials will dare to be associated with them."

Tuck's interest perked up. This could be the plan he was waiting for.

Flavin, wearing a sly grin, said, "Now listen up. You all know that the Boulder Water Ditch runs right below the Homestake." He folded his hands behind his back and slowly strolled around the table. "I hear the ditch's owners are hurting for money and willing to sell."

Bowlan cut in. "What has all this got to do with Hearst?"

Flavin waved his hand at Bowlan and said, "Take it easy, Archie. All we have to do is buy the Boulder Ditch and then take Hearst to court for spoiling the water. It shouldn't be hard to make a case. Then when we win, he won't be able to use his mills to process the Homestake ore."

Tuck took out his pocketknife and started cleaning his nails. He wished he had a better handle on what Flavin was talking about, but whatever it was there was no doubt it would add to George's troubles. Now all he had to do was remember the details.

Flavin slapped his hands together and started rubbing them back and forth. "We've got another problem though. Once we buy the water ditch, we've got to find a legitimate use for the water or the law won't let us keep it." He sat back down and poured himself another drink. "We all know Hearst won't buy water from us and since as it stands now, the Homestake is the only one needing water on that side of the district, we're going to have to find another use for it." He looked around the table. "Any ideas?"

Archie Bowlan scratched his head, leaned back in his chair, and stared at the ceiling. Suddenly he came forward, jumped to his feet, and said, "I know what we'll do. The whole world knows Deadwood's water supply ain't adequate. That was the main reason most of the town burned down. So—"

Gashwiler broke in. "Just what makes you think the City of Deadwood will buy water from us? I'm dead set against this idea. I don't see any use throwing good money after bad."

"Can I go on?" Archie gave Gashwiler a dirty look. "I didn't say I thought Deadwood would buy our water. That's why I'm saying we should give them free water for a year. That's long enough to show we're putting the water to good use." Archie's gaze wandered from one man to another. "One more thing. If you people don't want to throw in with me, I'll pull it off myself. I've got to stop Hearst."

Tuck knew his job had just gotten harder. George wasn't liked by a lot of people already. If he tried stopping the citizens of Deadwood from getting the free water they desperately needed the whole district would hate him. It might even put some more killers on his trail.

Pat Flavin said, "Let's take a vote. Who's willing to chip in?"

Tuck shifted his focus around the table. Archie Bowlan was the only man with a raised hand.

General Gashwiler got up from his chair and said, "Far as I'm concerned, each of us is on his own now. I'll pay my share of Flavin's bill up to this point, but not a penny more." He downed the rest of his bourbon and stomped out.

Archie Bowlan raised his hand again and said, "Look, Pat. I don't think it's fair to ask Bill Lardner or Captain Huron to go into this thing. They've already got enough problems. I'll buy the ditch on my own and if it helps them, all the better." Both men reached across the table and shook Archie's hand.

"Is there a part in this for me?" Tuck asked. "Or is my job over before it starts?"

Flavin turned to Bowlan. "What do you say, Archie? Are we going to need some help on the water deal?"

Bowlan thought for a second, looked at Tuck, and said, "We'll leave you on the payroll for now. I don't want anyone to know I'm connected with this till the whole thing's put to bed. You can help us dig up some folks willing to put the finger on Hearst and the Homestake for their terrible acts of pollution." He gave Tuck a smile and asked, "Think you can handle that, Tuck?"

Tuck nodded and said, "I need the money. Just tell me what to do, and I'll get it done."

Pat Flavin turned to Tuck and said, "Stick with me. I'll tell you what we need." Then he got up, looked at Archie Bowlan, and said, "If we don't have anything else to discuss, I'd like to call it a night. There's a poker game in the back room of the Silver Star and they're holding a seat for me."

Chapter Thirteen

George Hearst shifted the chaw of tobacco from his left cheek to his right. The pounding of mills, the yelling of workers, the hammering of carpenters, and the mingled smell of horse manure, fresh-cut lumber, and a variety of ethnic cooking permeated the air in Gold Run Gulch, the home of Lead City. This constant noise was why he loved to get away and spend time with Ira at the cabin. He had planned to stay a couple of more days, but helping Kelly out of this mess seemed much more important.

Besides, this time Charley Utter had gone too far. If a woman wanted to sell herself, that was her business. But making her do so against her will was another thing altogether. Almost as bad was the way he used his fists on the girls. No real man would ever do that. And it was even worse when an innocent young woman like Kelly was being battered.

George Hearst spit out his used-up chaw, removed a plug of Horseshoe from the bib of his overalls, and bit off a fresh chunk. He rolled the tobacco around in his mouth, working up a new supply of juice. Then he leaned over the sidewalk and spit into the dusty street before he turned and pushed open the door to Charley Utter's bawdy house.

Once inside he gave the crowded room a quick look around and headed for the bar. He thought he heard some-one call his name, but till he got his business done he was in no mood for conversation. George elbowed his way through the crowd, bellied up to the polished mahogany bar, and beckoned the bartender.

Soon as the bartender saw who it was, he put on a big grin and said, "Well, if it ain't old man Hearst. You out to spend some of the Homestake's money? You're in the right place—pick yourself a girl and Charley'll see that you get a good time." He sat a glass in front of George and reached for a bottle. "Bourbon, right? Tell you what. The first drink is on Charley."

George fought back the urge to wipe the smirk off the fat barkeep's face, but instead he quickly pushed back the glass and said, "Keep your rotgut booze. I'm here to see Charley Utter. If you know what's good for you, you'll go tell him that I am here and that we have business to dis-cuss."

The barkeep snarled and said, "You may be the big shot when it comes to the Homestake, but in here you're just another customer. You want to see Charley? Well, buy a few rounds of drinks and I may get him." He turned and strolled to the other end of the bar.

George clenched his fists and felt the sweat forming on his palms and between his fingers. Shoving his way to where the barkeep was standing, he reached across the bar and grabbed him by the sleeve garter. "You go get Utter now! Bring him out here or I'm going back there."

The barkeep's face turned a bright pink as he said, "I can't go back there now. He's taking a bath and he'll kill me if I bother him."

George turned loose the man's sleeve garter and said, "Well, Utter ain't going to kill me!" He quickly recalled Kelly's layout of the place, pushed aside the drape, rushed into the back hallway, and threw open the door to Charley's office. Sure enough, Charley was stretched out in a porcelain tub full of steaming water. Hearst went inside and kicked the door closed behind him.

Charley looked up. His mouth dropped open. His eyes got as big as silver dollars. "Who in the devil are you?" he asked. "And what are you doing here? I'll kill the jerk that let you in. Now get your carcass out of here!" All of a sudden his expression changed and he asked, "Say, ain't you George Hearst?"

George pointed his finger at Charley and said, "Glad you know who I am. Haul yourself out of that water and put some clothes on. We've got business."

Charley sat up straight. "No we don't. Go back to the bar and when I'm done you can tell me what's on your mind."

George marched to the edge of the tub, stared down at Charley Utter, and said, "You know you shouldn't talk tough to me. Why, I remember when you had nothing to wear but buckskins. And how you used to shovel horse manure out of that poor excuse of a livery stable in Georgetown, Colorado." From the expression on Charley's face, George knew he had hit a nerve. "If you hadn't teamed up with Wild Bill you'd still be up to your knees in dung."

"Those days are over," snarled Charley. "Ain't no cleaner man in the territory than me."

George squeezed his cud of tobacco between his jaw and worked up an ample supply of juice. When sure he had enough, he spit a glob of the disgusting-looking liquid into Charley's bathwater. Then with a grin that lit up his face, George said, "I'll bet you get out of there now."

Charley, with an expression of total disbelief, stared down at the spreading circle of tobacco juice. As it got closer and closer to his chest, panic filled his eyes. Grabbing the edges of the tub, he vaulted out of the water. He glared at George and said, "Why'd you do that?"

Angry as he was, George couldn't help laughing. "Charley, from the way you jumped, you'd think I threw a dia-mondback in that tub. Now, first cover yourself with that towel and then plant yourself on that chair."

Charley's mouth was jabbering like a magpie, but no sound was coming out. Shivering, he grabbed the towel and sat down. For some reason, he was no longer a tough guy.

Hearst dug deep into his overalls and pulled out a hand-ful of gold coins. One at a time, he dropped them at Char-ley's feet. A ringing thud followed each drop. When the twentieth coin hit the floor, George said, "I'm told that a young lady named Kelly Ryan owes you three hundred dollars. Now that account should be settled and you'll stay off her back." He handed Charley a paper and pencil. "Now, sign that receipt."

Suddenly a loud knock sounded on the door. "You all right, Charley?" Charley looked like he wasn't sure what he wanted to say, but finally he yelled, "I'll be out in a few minutes." He took the paper from George, signed it, and handed it back.

George checked the signature, folded the receipt, and stuck it back into his pocket. "There's one more thing, Charley. Kelly left her clothes here. She wants them back."

Charley squirmed in his chair and then said, "I don't have them. When she disappeared, the other girls split them up between them. There's nothing left. Besides, she owes me for the costume she stole."

George just looked at Charley and shrugged before he bent over and picked up seven gold coins. "In that case, I'll have to take back some of these for Kelly to buy new clothes. If you really want it, I'll see that you get what's left of that stupid costume."

"Why are you protecting that little killer? When the sher-iff gets hold of her for killing Joe Meeks, she won't need any clothes. That woman is a cold-blooded murderer. You should've seen what she did to poor old Joe."

George leaned down and stuck his face about two inches from Charley's nose and snarled, "Whatever she did to him, he deserved. She told me the whole story. How you hit her and forced her into that room with that snake you call poor old Joe. I going to leave you now, but you can bet that I'm not done with you." He turned and headed for the door. On his way past the tub, he sent another glob of tobacco juice splashing in the water. The sound of Charley Utter's cussing was music to George's ears.

When he got back to his hotel, George found letters from his wife, Phoebe, his partner Lloyd Tevis, and two plain envelopes. He read Phoebe's letter first and learned that, as usual, the main subject was the problems she was having with their son, Willie. If she'd stop babying him, maybe he'd grow up.

He found Lloyd's letter more interesting. Sufficient funding had been found to buy the machinery for two new stamp mills and they'd found a freight outfit willing to accept Homestake stock in payment for transporting them.

In the first unmarked envelope, he found a note from Tuck saying that he'd be at George's room that night with some important information. The other contained a notice from his mine superintendent, Sam McMaster, that John Smith, the Cornish foreman of the Homestake contract crew, had been arrested. John and some of his men were charged with killing Alex Frankenburg, the owner of a mill site Sam was trying to buy. Sam was asked that George meet with him and the company attorneys in Sam's office at three that afternoon. He checked his pocket watch: two o'clock. He had just enough time to grab a bite to eat before the meeting.

His lunch didn't go down well. He was worried about John and his crew. Everybody knew Frankenburg owned a claim that George needed for a stamp mill. It'd be easy to make a case that John and his men were acting on behalf of the Homestake. For a second, he wondered if the charges were true, but that was foolish. He knew he hadn't given any order to kill Frankenburg, and he was sure Sam hadn't either. This thing had to be settled in a hurry. The Homestake's popularity was dropping rapidly.

At three o'clock on the nose, George knocked on the door of McMaster's office. Almost immediately the door opened and standing there was McMaster, a tall, big-boned, young Irishman, thirty-eight years old, with a heavy mustache, and deepset eyes, with his right hand extended. George was very fond of this man, not only from his talents, but because he worked alone, an aspect Hearst never overlooked. George gave Sam's hand a quick shake and barged past him into the room. Seated at the polished conference table were the two Homestake attorneys, Corson and Thomas. Both had accompanied George to the Black Hills.

When no one seemed to want to be the first to speak, George looked at McMaster and said, "Well, I'm here like you wanted. Fill me in on the charges Smith and his men are accused of."

McMaster cleared his throat, then said, "About all we know for sure is that Alex Frankenburg was shot and killed on one of our claims. Sheriff Bullock claims he's found an eyewitness who says he saw Smith pull the trigger."

The wrinkles on Hearst's forehead turned into deep furrows. "Go on," he said.

"When the sheriff tried to arrest Smith, Smith's crew went to help him, forcing the sheriff to arrest the whole crew. As soon as I found out, I sent Corson and Thomas down to the jail." He glanced at the two attorneys. "They managed to get all but Smith and two others released. Smith is charged with murder and the other two as accessories. Judge Moody scheduled the arraignment for day after tomorrow."

George stared at Corson for a moment and then said, "Did you find out who the eyewitness is?"

"Yes, sir," said Corson. "He's a miner who used to work for Frankenburg."

George nodded. "Did you get Smith's side of the story?"

"He says he doesn't have a story, except to say he didn't do it."

George smiled and said, "If John Smith says he didn't do it, then he didn't do it. But there must be more to this whole blasted thing than you're telling me."

Thomas rose to his feet, faced Hearst and said, "Smith says they were all drinking in the Silver Star when Frankenburg started bad-mouthing you and the Homestake. Smith didn't like it and invited Frankenburg outside. He accepted and they stomped up the hill to the Golden Star Mill where they squared off."

Corson broke in and said, "Frankenburg took a swing at Smith and Smith ducked. At the exact same time, a shot rang out and Frankenburg went down. Then out of the blue, this attorney, Pat Flavin, stepped up and pointed at a pistol lying beside the body."

"Did Smith see the pistol?" asked George.

"Not before Flavin pointed it out," replied Corson.

"Okay. Tell me what happened next," said George.

"Flavin started yelling that he saw Smith drop the gun. Then he grabbed Smith's arm and tried to hold him. Smith's crew rushed for the crowd to break him from Flavin's grip. That's when the ruckus really started. It was going full force when the sheriff showed up."

"That's a lie!" said George as he slapped the table. "I've known Smith for years and I don't think he ever owned a gun in his life. This is a frame-up." He stared at the two attorneys. "I don't care what you have to do, or how much it costs, I'm expecting you two to make sure Smith and his men don't get hurt. If we look bad in the process, I don't give a hoot."

George got up and before starting for the door said, "Sam, keep me informed. Let me know what time the arraignment is. I want to be there."

George then went back to his room and waited for Tuck to come and fill him in on what he'd learned about Archie

Bowlan and the DeSmet's plans for stopping the Home-stake.

Two days later, George Hearst sauntered into the court-room and took a seat. Smith and his men were seated at a table in front of the bench. They were flanked by the two Homestake lawyers, Corson and Thomas. The prosecutor was seated alone to the right of the bar. Thomas turned and looked at George with a smile that told Hearst the lawyer had found a way to throw the balance in their favor.

Judge Moody, tall and slender in his black robes, entered through a door behind the bench. The bailiff shouted, "All rise." The judge took his seat. The bailiff took his and everyone else followed suit. The judge picked up his gavel and gave three quick taps, then said, "The court will come to order!" He looked at the prosecutor and asked, "Is the government ready to proceed?"

The prosecutor, a small hawk-nosed man with greasy hair plastered to his skull, looked sheepishly at the judge and asked in a whispered voice, "Your honor, may I approach the bench?"

George wondered what was going on. But he'd bet his two attorneys had a lot to do with the frustrated look on the prosecutor's face. Spotting an empty chair in the second row, George moved up front to make sure he didn't miss anything.

Judge Moody put down his gavel and said, "Would the defense attorneys like to join us?" Corson and Thomas moved alongside the prosecutor. Judge Moody leaned across the bench and asked in a low voice, "What's your problem?"

The prosecutor looked like he wanted to run and hide as he said, "Your honor, our eyewitness has disappeared. We've been looking for him since yesterday, but we can't find a trace of him. The government requests a week's post-ponement."

An annoyed frown formed on the judge's face. "Does the defense have any objections?"

Corson and Thomas glanced at each other for a second, then Corson said, "Yes, your honor, the defense most assuredly does. We've got three of our company's best miners locked in jail because of this trumped-up charge." He let his words sink in, then said, "With all due respect, we don't even know if this eyewitness ever existed. There were thirty or forty people at the scene; the government must have other witnesses they can call. The defense requests that we proceed."

George could feel an aura of confidence flowing from the defense team. They were the aggressors now.

Judge Moody stared at the prosecutor and asked, "Has the government other witnesses it can call?"

The prosecutor looked as if his wife just caught him kissing another woman. "We have one other witness, but it's my feeling that for justice to be done, we should be granted a postponement."

The judge gave him a wry smile, "Justice for whom. Certainly not the defendants." He gaveled the bench. "Request denied. Call your witness."

Pat Flavin was called and told how he spotted the gun lying by Frankenburg's body. "A gun only John Smith could've dropped," he said.

On cross examination, Thomas asked, "Mr. Flavin, did you see John Smith shoot Alex Frankenburg?"

Flavin folded his arms across his huge belly and said, "Well, I didn't actually see him pull the trigger, but it had to be him."

"Why?" asked Thomas.

"Because he was the only one close enough to have done it," Flavin answered.

Thomas paused and looked around the courtroom before asking, "Mr. Flavin, were you not next to the body when you spotted the gun?"

Flavin's expression was starting to show a strain. "Yes, I was. But I didn't shoot him."

"But you could have dropped the gun?" asked Thomas.

"That's ridiculous!" said Flavin. "I'm an attorney. An officer of the court. I wouldn't do something like that."

Thomas held up one finger and said, "Mr. Flavin. You didn't answer my question. Let's try it again. You could have dropped the gun, couldn't you?"

Flavin stared down at his sweating hands and said, "I suppose I could've but I didn't."

Thomas moved in front of the judge and said, "No further questions, your honor."

"Thank you, Mr. Thomas," said Judge Moody. "Mr. Prosecutor, call your next witness."

"The government rests."

"Does the defense wish to call witnesses?" asked Judge Moody.

Corson stood up and said, "We have no witnesses, your honor, but the defense does move that a verdict of not guilty be rendered. We maintain that the government has failed to establish that a crime has been committed."

George saw the judge glance in his direction and felt sorry for him. He had already asked Hearst for the job of Chief Council for the Homestake. If he granted this motion, everyone would say he did it in exchange for the job.

Finally the judge said, "Mr. Corson, your motion is temporally denied. It is true the government has not presented any direct evidence that the defendants committed the murder. But there is no doubt that a man was shot. Furthermore, there is no evidence that the shooting was accidental. Therefore we have to assume that a crime has been committed. I'm releasing the defendants on their own recognition. If the government can come up with viable evidence to connect these men or any other men with the crime, I'll reopen the case."

George looked down at his shoes to hide his smile. Judge Moody had found a way out of his predicament.

"Now," said Judge Moody. "If there is no further business before this court, this session is closed."

As George watched Moody hurry through the back door, he wondered if the judge had ever considered taking up acting.

Chapter Fourteen

The sun stood directly overhead as Tuck coaxed his rented chestnut-colored horse across the narrow stream running between two large beaver ponds. The horse's hooves sounded like pulling corks out of wine bottles in the soft mushy earth between the dams. But only a few more feet and he'd be on the tail to Ira's cabin.

Tuck couldn't remember the last time he'd been so eager to see someone. It had only been a week since he said good-bye to Kelly, but it seemed like a month or more. The fact that he was bringing good news made him feel even more anxious.

Reining up in front of the cabin, Tuck let out a yell. By the time he'd swung down from the horse, he saw Ira standing in the doorway, a big smile across his chocolate-colored face. "Where's Kelly?" shouted Tuck. "I've got good news for her."

Ira, his smile turning to a grin, shuffled forward with an outstretched hand. "Well, can you imagine that? My good friend don't even say hello to old Ira. Sure ain't hard to see who brings you out here."

Ira took the reins and led the horse to a little corral behind the woodpile. Tuck trailed close behind as he asked, "But where is she? She's still here, ain't she?" A knot started forming in his gut.

Ira tilted his head and gave Tuck a sideways glance as he said, "Pull in a bit. Kelly's fine. She and Armstrong went up the draw to catch some fish for lunch. She'll be back before long."

Tuck breathed a bit easier. "She's gone fishing?" he asked. "How'd she ever learn to fish?"

"That girl's got a lot of secrets," said Ira, opening the gate. "What she told me is that when she was a young girl in Ireland, her grandfather took her fishing all the time. And she learned to love it." He led the horse into the corral and tied him to a rail. "Personally, I don't go much for fish, but it makes her feel like she's pulling her own weight. This past week, almost every day we've had trout for breakfast or lunch."

Tuck's only thought was of going up the draw to look for her, but he didn't want to appear too eager. "We'll have some time to talk while we're waiting," he said. "How's she getting along?" He untied a large package wrapped in brown paper from behind the cantle and laid it on the ground.

As Tuck was doing that, Ira uncinched the chestnut's saddle and hung it on the top rail. He then limped across the corral, forked up a hefty load of hay, and dumped it at the horse's front feet.

Satisfied that the horse's well-being was taken care of, Tuck lifted the package and followed Ira inside the cabin where he went directly to the stove and slid the coffeepot over the fire. "You ready for a cup of my good coffee?"

"Sure am," said Tuck as he dropped the package on the settee and took a seat at the table. "Now are you going to tell me how Kelly is?"

Ira took a hard look at Tuck, grinned, and said, "I just told you, she's fine. In fact, Armstrong's taken a real liking to her. So much so that he hardly pays me any attention anymore. I guess that goes to show you he's got good taste. She's a real fine girl." Ira set two cups on the table. "She's very frightened though, and I've got a notion she finds it hard to trust anyone. That is except for you. All she talks about is how much you've done for her."

Tuck pondered Ira's words for a second before saying, "She'll get over that. I think she's been kicked around a lot. But now that George is helping her, she's sure to get on her feet again. And it won't take long, either. I wouldn't doubt that in no time she'll be setting out to conquer the world." Tuck thought over his words and wondered if he really wanted her to be so successful. She'd become real important to his life and a good-sized chunk of each day was spent thinking about her. He hated to imagine how it would be without her. It was just too bad he was so much older than she was.

They finished their coffee and went outside to get a breath of fresh air and wait for Kelly and Armstrong to return. While Ira sat down on the large block of wood he used for chopping, Tuck eased himself onto the cabin's front step, leaned back on his elbows, stretched out his legs, and crossed them at the ankles. He'd just gotten comfortable when he heard a frantic combination of barking, howling, and what sounded like calls for help.

Ira stood and faced the direction of the noise. "That's Armstrong," he said. "And from the sound of it, something ain't right."

Tuck stood at his side for a second, then said, "I'm going to find out what's wrong." He started toward the draw.

Ira grabbed his arm. "Wait a minute. Take my rifle from over the fireplace. Be careful. It's loaded."

Tuck dashed inside, grabbed the 30-30 Marlin, moved quickly to the kitchen table, grabbed a handful of cartridges, and took off running. Was it his imagination or did the barking sound more desperate? He had to hurry. He was sure his Kelly was in trouble.

The trail was strewn with large boulders, logs, and dead tree branches. Even under normal circumstances, it would've been difficult to move at a fast pace, but he couldn't risk slowing down. He took to jumping over the stumps and jagged rocks as he sped toward Armstrong's desperate call. Then he heard Kelly yelling, "Ira! Help!"

The fear in her scream gave him a new burst of energy. On up the draw he charged, through thick brush and over fallen trees. He was getting closer. The screams and barking were growing louder and louder. When he figured he was just about there, he stopped running and moved forward with caution.

He worked his way over a small rise, and spotted Kelly standing on top of a huge moss-covered boulder. Ten feet or more above the ground, she tightly gripped her fishing pole, the line still hanging from its tip. Armstrong's growling was coming from the far side of the rock. Suddenly from around the boulder came a huge grizzly. On the bear's heels came Armstrong with teeth bared, saliva flowing from his mouth, and the look of kill showing in his eyes. The bear stopped and swirled around to face Armstrong.

Fear surged through Tuck's body. Was Ira's rifle heavy enough to kill an animal that large? If he just wounded the bear, would he ever get Kelly down off that rock? Should he run and try to get the bear to follow so she could escape? He knew the bear could outrun him, but if he could just give Kelly the time she needed to escape, whatever happened to him would be worth it. But he thought about the fight with the miner and had a feeling she'd come after the bear instead of running away. No, his only option was to shoot, but he had to make sure he hit a vital organ.

The bear reared on his hind feet and challenged Armstrong. The dog retreated a few feet and then turned back to the bear that was now resting his front paws on the side of the rock and groping for the top. Surprisingly Kelly leaned over and swung the fishing pole, striking the growling bear square of the nose. At the same time, Armstrong sneaked back in and snapped at the bear's hind legs. The bear let out a loud grunt and dropped down on all four paws. Armstrong once again retreated, his lips peeled back to expose a fearsome set of teeth as he once again faced the grizzly. The bear attacked again. Armstrong ran around the rock with the bear in hot pursuit. Kelly moved along the edge, keeping the fishing pole between her and the old bear.

This time when the bear came back into view and raised up on his hind legs to try to get at Kelly, Tuck stepped into the open. His palms were damp with sweat. His body felt too heavy for his legs. He raised the rifle and aimed at a spot directly behind the bear's left shoulder. He squeezed he trigger and saw a puff of dust rise from the spot he was aiming at. But, instead of going down, the grizzly turned and headed toward Tuck.

With Kelly's screaming and Armstrong's barking echoing in his ears, Tuck stood his ground and aimed at the oncoming bear's chest. Bang! Bang! Bang! Blood spurted but the bear kept coming. Tuck squeezed off two more shots, turned, and started to run. He glanced over his shoulder and then stopped running. The bear was down. Armstrong darted in and sank his teeth into the huge animal's neck. The bear didn't move a muscle.

Tuck staggered to the nearest tree and sat down with his back leaning against it and took several deep breaths. His legs felt froze in place as he watched Kelly climb down from the rock and come running in his direction. In one hand she still carried her fishing pole, in her other a string of trout.

"Tuck!" she screamed. Her voice sounded as if she was crying and laughing at the same time. "Would you believe it? I was praying you would come and rescue me from that awful bear. How'd you get here? Did you see the way Armstrong was protecting me?"

Tuck rose to his feet, leaned the rifle against the tree, and moved toward her. When they were within a few feet of each other, Kelly dropped her pole and the fish. As they met, she wrapped her arms around him, and said, "Oh, Tuck. How I've missed you."

He wanted to tell her he felt the same way. But he couldn't believe she really felt for him as he wanted her to. It was natural for her to feel obligated to him. After all, she had no one else to turn to. He had to admit though that her arms wrapped around him made him feel very special and would have loved to return her embrace. Things between them were moving too fast. He reached behind him and gently took her wrists and broke her hold on him. "We'd better get back to Ira," he said. "I'm sure he's worried about you."

His words changed her welcoming smile and gleaming eyes to a frown and misty vision.

Pretending he didn't notice, Tuck retrieved the rifle as Kelly picked up her pole and fish. Then with Armstrong at their side, they headed back down the draw toward the cabin.

As they moved along, Tuck had trouble keeping his eyes off Kelly. She was dressed in a knee-length doeskin dress with a red-beaded design running across her shoulders and down the sleeves. Her rust-colored hair was parted in the middle and braided. Bows of green ribbon held the braids together. The bruises that had marked her face were gone. In their place, Tuck noticed tiny freckles sprinkled across her petite nose and slightly tanned cheeks. For some reason he felt like a boy back on the farm where he and Mary Lou grew up.

When Kelly caught him staring, she asked, "Do you like my dress? I made it myself. Ira showed me what to do, but I did all the work myself." She stood before him, extended one foot forward and curtsied.

Tuck knew he was blushing but didn't know how to hide it. It was amazing how the little things she did affected him. "It's a nice dress," he said. "You did a great job. But didn't you get the clothes Mrs. Robinson bought for you?"

She nodded. "Yes, I got them and they're very nice. They'll be great when I get back to town, but they're not too practical for traipsing around the woods."

Suddenly Armstrong let out a short howl and took off down the trail. Tuck reached out, grabbed Kelly's arm, and said, "Might be more trouble. Let's wait a minute and see what's got him excited."

With her arm still in his grasp, they stood watching the spot they'd last seen Armstrong. Within seconds, Ira came limping around the bend. Kelly saw him and yelled, "Ira! Look who's here. Tuck saved me from a big bear. He was so brave and wonderful."

With everything now safe, they all sat down. While Ira rested, Tuck told his part of the story and Kelly told hers.

Ira wrapped his arm around Kelly, and said, "I'll bet that old bear scared the life out of you. But chances are she was only after your fish. Most bears love fish, ants, grubs, berries, nuts, and roots. Very few of them are meat eaters."

Tuck stared at the old man. "You mean I really didn't have to kill the bear? How'd you know it's a female?"

"You did the right thing," said Ira. "With Kelly whipping her with that fishing pole and Armstrong biting her legs, that old she-devil was probably mad enough to do anything. Besides that, we can use the skin and meat."

Tuck stared up the trail to where the bear lay stretched out. "But you still haven't told me how you know it's a female."

Ira stretched his hand out to Tuck and motioned for him to help him up. "The silver tips," said Ira. "Males are more of a chocolate brown. But she's a big one. I think you two had better go back to the cabin and get that horse. I'll start skinning her out."

Ira opened the blade of his pocketknife and stropped it across his boot. "This'll do to get me started. When you come back, bring the butcher knives from the kitchen." He limped up the trail toward the fallen bear.

* * *

A few hours later, Tuck swigged down the last of his beer, pushed away from the table, and said, "First time I ever ate bear meat. Can't say I'd trade a good beef steak for it, but it sure hit the spot tonight."

Kelly moved behind Tuck and put her hands on his shoulders. She lowered her face next to his and said, "When do I get to see what's in the package?"

Tuck had a strong urge to quickly turn and kiss her cheek, but instead, he got up and carried his plate to the sink. "Let's help Ira clean up first." He rubbed his hands together as he said, "After you see what I've brought you, I'll tell both of you everything that happened."

Kelly grabbed the dishrag. "Let's hurry up, I can't wait to hear what you've got to say."

When the dishes were put away and the floor swept, Tuck tossed her the bundle and said, "Here ya go. Open it up."

Kelly took the package and dropped to the rug in front of the fireplace. When she had trouble untying the knots, Tuck took out his knife, cut the twine, and let the paper fall away. "Oh, Tuck!" she said. "It's my clothes—even my cape." She jumped up, draped the cape over her shoulder, and spun in a circle. "This was my grandmother's. When we left Ireland, she gave it to my mother to hold till I got big enough to wear it." A tiny tear appeared in the corner of her eye. She wiped it away with her hand and asked, "But how did you get everything out of that horrible place?"

"You can thank George and Trixie for that," Tuck said as he sat down on one of the bent-willow chairs and explained how George paid off Charley Utter for Kelly's transportation and then took back part of the money because he'd given her clothes away.

Kelly gave Tuck a quizzical look and asked, "But if he gave them away, how'd you get them?"

Tuck smiled. "George gave me the money he'd taken from Charley Utter and then Trixie helped me buy every-

G. Sam Carr

thing back from the girls." He took her two hands in his and said, "Now for the big news. George wants me to stay out here for three or four days, then I'm to bring you back into town with me. In the meantime, he'll be taking care of the charges against you."

A dead calm came over her. "Can he really do that?"

Tuck nodded. "I'd bet my life on it."

Chapter Fifteen

Since dawn, Kelly had paced the floor of her hotel room. Every third time she passed the window, she stopped, edged the shade aside, and peeked down at the street below. She wasn't sure what she expected to see, but for some reason just looking made her feel better. Only Tuck and George knew she was here. It was pitch black when Tuck sneaked her into town and up to the room next to George's. Tuck said over and over again that she was as safe here as at Ira's cabin. If that was so, she should be able to relax, but try as she might, she couldn't. She tried going to sleep, but all she did was toss and turn. Finally she gave up and got out of bed. She'd been pacing ever since.

As much as Tuck assured her she was safe in the room, every time she heard a noise she worried it was Charley Utter or the sheriff coming to get her. George was certain he'd get her charges dropped, but until it happened she'd be on pins and needles. On the other hand, there were times when she wondered if she really wanted them dropped. She liked living out at the cabin. But she couldn't stay with Ira forever, and Tuck had his own life to live. For the first time since she left her grandparents behind in Ireland, she'd found people she loved and trusted. Now she stood the chance of being all alone again.

Ira had made a comment that she and Tuck would make a fine couple, but Tuck just shrugged it off by saying something about her finding a young man her own age. The fact was she didn't want a younger man—or any other man. If she couldn't have Tuck, she didn't want anybody.

Suddenly a knock on the door interrupted her thoughts. She held her breath, not moving a muscle. A knot twisted in her gut. But then she heard George's voice, saying, "Kelly, can you let me in?"

She paused for a second to let her hands stop shaking enough for her to pull back the bolt and open the door a crack. When she saw the long beard wrapped around a warm smile, she knew she was safe.

George pushed open the door and stepped quickly into the room. After closing and rebolting the door behind him, he said, "I got to thinking you must be about ready for some breakfast. We'll go downstairs. It won't be as good as Ira makes, but I eat there all the time and the food isn't bad."

Kelly stared at the old man, shook her head, and said, "I don't know. I'm hungry, but are you sure someone won't recognize me?"

"What if they do?" he said, smiling. "I won't let anybody hurt you. Besides, by this afternoon it's all going to be over."

Kelly thought for a minute, looked down at the floor, and said softly, "Maybe I should skip breakfast."

George reached down and put his leatherlike fingertips under her chin and lifted her head to where she was looking him in the eye. "You really are scared, aren't you?" he asked. "I'll tell you what we'll do. I've got a table and chairs in my rooms. I'll have the kitchen send something up. Will that make you feel better? How about some griddlecakes and bacon?"

A warm smile broke out on Kelly's face. "That sounds

good. Thank you." She turned, walked to the window and peeked out. Then suddenly she spun around and asked, "George, do I really have to go to court?"

George moved to her side. "It's best you do, Kelly. My lawyers say we can get this behind you if we find a judge to rule that you're not guilty. They don't think you'll have to take the stand, but if things aren't going right, you might have to. But still everything will work out."

Her stomach churned at the thought of being in the witness chair and everybody looking at her. "Oh, George," she said. "If you only knew how I feel about seeing Charley Utter again."

Hearst nodded and put his right arm around her shoulders. "I think I know, but you can't run and hide forever. But don't you worry about Charley Utter. I can tell you for sure that he's going to have a lot more on his mind than you." He used his left hand to remove a dribble from his mouth. "There's something else I must warn you about. When you see Tuck in court, make like you don't know who he is. Nobody in this town except you, me, and Ira knows he works for me."

Kelly nodded and said, "Tuck told me what he's doing for you. But why is he going to be at the trial?"

Hearst grinned through tobacco-stained teeth and said, "If it comes about that we need him, we'll call him as a witness. But only if things get out of line." He paused. "Now don't you start worrying. We don't expect any problems."

She looked into his eyes and said, "I hope you're right."

He gave her a squeeze and said, "I guarantee I'm right. Now let's go get us some griddlecakes."

When it came time to leave the hotel, her fears were running rampant again. Even hiding her face by keeping the edges of her cape pulled tight didn't help. All the way to the courthouse, her hands sweated and the hair on the back of her neck stood stiff. Holding tight to George's arm, she walked into the courthouse with her knees shaking and feeling as if she was going to faint.

George led her down the aisle and sat her at a table facing the judge's bench. A good-looking man with an Abe Lincoln beard came up to George and shook hands. "Kelly," George said, "this is Dan Thomas. He'll be your attorney."

Kelly tried to smile as George said, "There ain't no finer lawyer in this country." But in her heart she wondered if he was just trying to make her feel good. Hoping to hide her thoughts, she looked around the overcrowded room and recognized several faces. At first she wondered if they were there to help or hurt her, but then she knew she was being stupid. Trixie, Mrs. Robinson, and Mrs. Hayes were sitting together. They were her friends and would never hurt her. A couple of rows back of them Tuck was busy talking to a dirty-looking fat man. Tuck would never hurt her. She didn't know the fat man but assumed he was Tuck's friend.

At a table on the other side of the aisle sat Charley Utter dressed in his fancy black broadcloth trousers and Prince Albert coat. Unlike the others, the sight of him sent a chill running up her spine. She didn't recognize the man with Charley, but in the first row behind them she did recognize his bartender and piano player.

Feeling a hand on her shoulder, Kelly twisted around and looked up into the kind eyes of George. He smiled and said, "Don't worry, honey. It'll be over before you know it."

"I hope so," she said. "Who's the man with Charley Utter?"

George glanced in Charley's direction and said, "That's Brent Ford, U.S. Attorney. We'd better be quiet now. I think the trial is about to start."

She turned back around and watched the door behind the judge's bench open. Judge Moody, dressed in a long black robe, entered the room. At that very same moment, a man wearing a badge jumped up and yelled, "All rise."

Everyone did as the man ordered. Then when the judge

took his seat, everybody except Kelly sat down. Mr. Thomas tugged at her sleeve and whispered, "You can sit down now."

The judge pounded his gavel and said, "The court will come to order. The district court of the Black Hills, Dakota Territory is now in session. Mr. Ford, are you ready to proceed?"

"Yes, your honor."

The judge shifted his gaze toward Kelly. "Is the defense ready?"

Mr. Thomas rose to his feet and said, "The defense is ready."

After picking up a sheet of paper in front of him, the judge looked out at the rows and people and read aloud, "There will be two pieces of business conducted here today. The first is The People vs. Kelly Ryan on the charge of murder. The second is a civil complaint. When the murder trial is concluded, I'll disclose the nature of the civil complaint. We'll now seat a jury."

Kelly wished she knew more about what they were doing. The clerk called a name. A man came forward and took the witness stand. Mr. Thomas and Mr. Ford took turns asking the man questions. Over and over the same thing happened. Some were excused; the others took seats in the jury box.

When twelve men were seated, the judge announced the trial would commence. He looked at Charley's table and asked, "Does the prosecutor have an opening statement?"

Mr. Ford rose from his chair. "I do, your honor." He turned toward the jury. "Gentlemen, the prosecution will prove beyond a reasonable doubt that the defendant, Miss Kelly Ryan, murdered, in cold blood, Mr. Joe Meeks, a fine upstanding visitor from San Francisco."

Upon hearing the words, Kelly jumped to her feet and started to scream at the prosecutor. Thomas grabbed her arm and said, "Miss Ryan, you must remain seated. If you don't, it's going to be much harder to defend you." Kelly sat back down hoping the jury didn't believe what Mr. Ford had said.

The judge looked to Mr. Thomas. "Does the defense wish to say something?"

"Not at this time, your honor," said Thomas.

"Very well. Mr. Ford, call your first witness."

Charley Utter was called and took an oath to tell the truth, the whole truth, and nothing but the truth. Kelly gritted her teeth and felt blood rush to her face.

Mr. Ford asked him if he owned a business in Lead City. "Yes," Charley said. "I own a social club for the entertainment of the good people of Lead City."

Ford rubbed his hands together and asked, "Do you know the accused, Kelly Ryan? If you see her in the court, would you point her out."

Kelly lowered her eyelids to where she could barely see the smirk on Charley's face as he pointed in her direction.

"Mr. Utter, please tell the jury what transpired on the night of August tenth."

Charley shifted in his chair, stared at the jury and said, "It really pains me to talk about it." He paused long enough to frown and rub his right sleeve across his eyes. "The way I remember it is that Joe Meeks came into my place through the back door. I knew Joe from my days in Colorado. Joe was self-conscious because he only had one eye and had to wear a patch over the empty socket where his other eye used to be. I didn't think nothin' of it when he asked to use my office, or when he asked me to have someone bring him a bottle."

Charley looked down at his feet and shook his head. "Miss Ryan there"—he looked at Kelly—"happened to be near the bar so I sent her in with a bottle for poor old Joe."

Kelly pulled on her attorney's sleeve. "He's lying. Can't you do something?"

Thomas put his forefinger to his lips and said, "Shush."

Shushing was the last thing she wanted to do, but she kept quiet as Charley went on to say, "After twenty minutes or so, she hadn't come out so I went in to see what was going on. That's when I found poor old Joe stretched out with a bullethole in his head. His pockets were turned inside out. The girl was nowhere in sight. It was obvious she had killed and robbed him. The back door was open so she must have escaped through there."

This time it was just too much. Kelly jumped up and yelled, "That's a lie! Why don't you say what really happened?"

Knock, knock, knock went the gavel. "Mr. Thomas, please keep your client under control or I'll find her in contempt of court."

The judge's attitude made Kelly even madder, but she looked at the expression on his face and figured it was best not to test him. She eased back into her chair and hung her head. Tears formed in the corners of her eyes. Why did she come here? She should have stayed with Ira.

When it was his turn, Mr. Thomas went to work on Charley. Kelly soon realized what George meant about him being the best in the country. With every question, he forced Charley to reveal more of the truth. He admitted that she was working to pay him back the money he'd advanced for her transportation. He even admitted that she had wanted to quit on the first day when she realized she hadn't been hired as an actress.

Time after time, Ford objected. Time after time, the judge overruled him. Kelly felt like applauding when, with each question, Charley lost more of his smugness. He squirmed in his chair and beads of sweat formed on his forehead. Finally Mr. Thomas had no more questions. Climbing down from the witness chair, Charley stared at Kelly with a look that sent shivers down her spine.

Mr. Ford then called the piano player trying to verify what Charley said on direct examination. But Mr. Thomas tore into him just as bad as he had Charley. Kelly relaxed enough to twist around and look at George. He had a big smile and an aura of confidence showed in his eyes. She'd like to turn around again to see what Tuck was doing, but thought better of it and concentrated on the trial.

As its next witness, the prosecution called the bartender. When Ford asked him what had happened, he started telling the version of the events as they actually occurred. Ford tried to stop him. The judge told him to continue. Kelly was elated. Instead of backing Charley, the barkeep was destroying him. When he finished, Mr. Thomas didn't even bother to cross-examine.

The prosecution rested and Kelly breathed a sigh of relief. As his first witness, Mr. Thomas called Trixie to the stand. She also told everything as it actually happened. Under cross-examination, the prosecutor tried to get her to change her story, but she didn't waiver. Kelly smiled. Indeed, Trixie was a true friend.

When her attorney called Mrs. Robinson and Mrs. Hayes, they both described Kelly's condition that night. For some reason neither one of them mentioned Tuck. She had a hunch that George had his hand in briefing them. She knew that Ira was right when he told her that George Hearst could do whatever he had a mind to. She turned and smiled at George. He returned her smile with a quick wink.

Soon as the jury filed out, Kelly saw Trixie, Mrs. Robinson, and Mrs. Hayes pushing their way through the crowd toward her. "Kelly, you look beautiful," said Mrs. Robinson. "Sure a lot different than the last time I saw you. The dress looks much better than my son's old black suit."

After Kelly thanked Mrs. Robinson for her help that night and for the dresses she had sent out to the cabin, she grabbed Trixie and wrapped her arms around her. As they embraced in a tight hug, Kelly thanked her for rounding up her old clothes, especially her grandmother's cape. Trixie beamed.

When Kelly felt a tug on her arm, she looked down and saw it was Mrs. Hayes. "Hey, don't forget me," the short, heavyset, old woman pleaded.

Kelly quickly bent down and gave Mrs. Hayes a big hug

as she said, "I could never forget you. But tell me, have you found a place to stay after the fire?"

Mrs. Hayes's eyes lit up. "You mean you don't know?"

"Know what?" Kelly asked.

The old woman lowered herself onto a chair, looked up at Kelly and said, "It was about three or four days after the fire. I'd managed to buy an old tent and set it up where my house used to be. Actually business was very good. All the men working on rebuilding the town bought fruit from me. But then the strangest thing happened."

"Nothing bad, I hope?" asked Kelly.

A big smile crossed Mrs. Hayes's wrinkled, weathered face. "Oh, no! Like I said, it was a few days after the fire when this well-dressed man paid me a visit. You could've knocked me over with a feather duster when he said, 'I've been hired to rebuild your house and fruit stand.' I told him I couldn't afford to rebuild right now, but he then said everything had been paid for."

"Really?" asked Kelly.

"Sure enough. The next day a bunch of carpenters showed up with a wagonload of lumber. Within a week, those men built me a beautiful new house with six bedrooms for the children and a new fruit stand with shelves and everything. They couldn't find another red awning so now the stand is covered with a green one. But . . ."

Kelly remembered the expression on George's face when she told him about Mrs. Hayes and how she helped homeless women and children. "Have you found out who paid for it?"

Mrs. Hayes shook her head. "Nope. At first I tried. I'd really like to thank whoever it was, but I haven't been able to find a clue."

Kelly smiled to herself. She was sure who it was.

Then the judge's door opened and he stepped up to his bench. The clerk shouted, "All rise."

Judge Moody sat down, gave three quick taps with his gavel, and said, "The court will come to order." He glanced

G. Sam Carr

at the clerk. "Bring the jury back in." He waited for them to take their seats before saying, "I understand you have reached a decision?"

A frail little man in the front row stood up and said, "We have, your honor."

"Please give us your verdict."

Kelly felt that old familiar knot forming in her stomach.

The little man cleared his throat and said, "We the jury find the defendant not guilty."

Spectators started cheering. Kelly collapsed into the arms of Mr. Thomas. Judge Moody frantically pounded his gavel. When the crowd settled a bit, he said, "This court is still in session. If I have to, I'll clear the room." Still it took several more seconds and many more knocks before order was fully restored. He thanked and excused the jury then declared that all warrants for Kelly's arrest were null and void. She was free to come and go as she pleased. He gave three more taps with the gavel before saying. "I will now hear the civil complaint. Mr. Utter, please stand before the bench."

Charley rose and walked slowly toward the judge. Obviously he wasn't very cocky now. Or very scary either. Kelly thought she heard some bitterness in the judge's voice when he said, "Mr. Utter. I have a petition signed by more than thirty residents of Lead City complaining about the nature of the establishment you're maintaining in their city." He picked up the paper, leaned over his bench, and waved it in front of Charley's face. "For your information, most of these fine people are present in court and willing to testify."

Kelly was on the edge of her chair. It was good to watch Charley squirm. She almost laughed at the way he flinched when the judge gestured toward the spectators.

The judge gave Charley a contemptible stare and went on saying, "Mr. Utter, these folks are ready to describe every aspect of your business; from the cancan dance to the shots of tea the girls are forced to drink and charge the customers for whiskey."

A roar of "yeas" from the audience sent the judge reaching for his gavel, but order returned without his having to use it. He fixed his stare on Charley again and said, "From the testimony we just heard in Miss Ryan's trial, it really doesn't matter how high the girls kick or what they're expected to drink." He leaned forward, his jaws tight. "The point is: you're permitting gambling, drinking, boisterous talk, and the herding of men and women together like animals. Do you have any evidence to present that contradicts what these folks are charging?"

Charley's face was red as blood as he said, "I'm not the only saloon in Lead City."

"That's true," said the judge. "The difference is that the others hold the line. So because of the indiscretions outlined in the petition and your lack of facts to contradict the facts, I believe you are indeed maintaining a public nuisance." A sudden burst of applause prevented Kelly from hearing the judge's final words.

The judge gaveled the room back to order and said, "Therefore, it's the order of this court that within the next twenty-four hours you close your place of business. Failure to do so will result in issuing an arrest order for contempt of court and you can bet your last dollar that I'll throw the book at you. However, if you follow my instructions, I'll sentence you to one hour of confinement in the city jail and fine you fifty dollars. In addition you are to pay all court costs." Before Charley had a chance to respond, the judge said, "This case is closed."

Charley Utter turned and rushed up the aisle. Loud jeers and catcalls followed him out the door.

When Kelly turned to watch Charley, she found George waiting to help her with her cape. "We have to hurry," he said. "There's someone outside who wants to meet you." Before she could ask any questions, George had her arm and was leading her out. When they emerged from the courthouse, George stopped and said, "Here he comes now."

Kelly looked and saw a man of medium build, wearing

tails, skin-tight trousers, and a silk top hat coming toward them. Snow-white spats covered his ankles and the sun flashed off the toes of his patent leather shoes. In one hand he carried a fancy walking stick and in the other a long slim unlit cigar. A friendly smile occupied the space below his pointed nose.

George yelled out, "Jack, you old reprobate, glad you could make it."

The man shook George's hand and said, "I didn't come to see you. I came to meet this lovely young lady." He took Kelly's hand, brought it to his lips and kissed it. "You must be the actress, Kelly Ryan. George tells me you spent some time as Lotta Crabtree's understudy."

The man's voice and the distinct way he pronounced each word fascinated Kelly. She knew she was talking to a gifted actor. She gently removed her hand, batted her eyelashes and said, "As a matter of fact, I was. But Lotta was such a trouper, she never missed a performance, so I decided that if I wanted to stay in the theater, I'd better go off on my own—"

George broke in and trying to put on airs said, "Miss Kelly Ryan, I'd like you to meet Mr. Jack Langrishe, a good friend and head of the Langrishe Theater Group."

Jack winked at Kelly and said, "George, we may be friends, but that doesn't give you the right to interrupt when I'm discussing theater with a beautiful woman. Miss Ryan, if you are so inclined, it would be my pleasure to have you join Mrs. Langrishe and me for dinner. It will give us a chance to discuss your joining our little group."

Kelly couldn't believe her ears. Was she dreaming? Was all this possible? All of a sudden everything seemed to be going her way. She curtsied and said, "I'd be delighted to be your guest."

"Very well," he said. "I'll have a carriage pick you up at seven." He spun around and walked away with movements so smooth he gave the appearance of floating.

Chapter Sixteen

When Tuck got to the cabin, he poured himself a cup of steaming coffee, pulled out a chair, and took a seat at the table. He'd been on the trail since before dawn. Renting a horse was out of the question, primarily because the hostler at the livery stable had a tendency to ask too many questions. Besides, George always walked and would kid the pants off him if he hired a horse without a good reason. The trip was long, but now the smell of Ira's coffee made it seem worthwhile. Tuck tried sipping his coffee. It was too hot. He put down the cup and watched Ira limp to the stove and pour himself a cup. On his slow trip back to the table, Ira smiled at Tuck and asked, "You want some breakfast now?"

Hoping to make the coffee cool faster, Tuck poured some into his saucer and blew on it. After he slurped a sip, he said, "I'm hungry enough to eat that old she-bear, but I can wait till George gets here." Satisfied with the results, Tuck downed another saucer full, then said, "He'll show up before long. His note said he'd be here early."

Ira nodded and lowered himself onto the chair opposite Tuck. "Have you seen Kelly?" he asked.

Tuck smiled and said, "Matter of fact, I have. Jack Langrishe has a play called *The Banker's Daughter* running at the Opera House. Jack plays the banker and Kelly plays his daughter." Tuck took some more coffee. "It's about this banker who loses all his money and the daughter marries a much older man. I went last night and was really surprised. Kelly's really a great actress. I had no idea."

Ira slid back his chair, stared at Tuck, and in a harsh voice said, "There's a lot about Kelly you don't see."

Now what did he mean by that? And why was Ira looking at him that way? It almost seemed that he was mad about something. Finally he said, "Ira, did I do something wrong?"

Ira limped to the stove, turned and faced Tuck. "You really don't know, do you? Why, it's plain as the nose—"

Armstrong jumped to his feet, threw his ears forward, and ran to the door. His tail was wagging like the wings of a hummingbird.

As he hurried to the door, Ira's frown was replaced by a giant smile. "That must be George," he said.

Hearst barged into the room, threw his old hat on the settee, and headed for the coffeepot. "Let's have some breakfast," he said. "Then we'll get down to business. Don't like talkin' on an empty stomach."

Tuck was amazed at how much and how fast George could eat. In less than twenty minutes he'd downed a man-sized steak, four eggs, fried potatoes, and several slices of bread. After draining his third cup of coffee, he got up, stretched his arms, and said, "Time to get started." He turned to Ira. "You need any help cleaning up?"

Ira acted like he was thinking, then said, "Yes. One of you can sweep the floor and do the dishes. The other can wash the windows and maybe do some laundry."

George's expression left no doubt he'd received an answer he'd never expected. Suddenly Ira started laughing, and said, "Now you know I don't need help. You and Tuck do what you've got to do. Don't worry about me."

Tuck smiled at the way the two old men badgered each other. It was obvious how much they really liked one another. No wonder they were the best of friends. Tuck was sure there wasn't a thing in the world that one wouldn't do for the other.

Then George turned to Tuck, and said, "What say we go outside and walk off this breakfast? I'll let you in on what I have in mind."

Tuck followed George outside and fell in beside him, the old man's long legs matching Tuck's step for step. When they got down to the spring, George kneeled down and took a long drink of the cold gurgling water. With his thirst satisfied, he got up, wiped his mouth on his sleeve, and took a seat on a downed tree trunk.

When Tuck sat down beside him, George slapped him on the knee and said, "Only got a few more things to take care of. If they go as planned, we should be back in Frisco next spring."

"Sounds good to me," said Tuck, not really sure of what he was saying. But nevertheless he knew they still had work to do. "What's our next step?"

George grinned, then said, "For one thing, I bought the Foster Water Ditch." His grin got wider. "That's the ditch that runs right past the DeSmet mine."

So thought Tuck as he asked, "You going to trade it for the Boulder Ditch?"

"Heck, no. I got hold of the Deadwood City officials and offered to supply them with an unlimited supply of free water."

Tuck laughed. "You're too much. But what is Deadwood going to do now that they can get water from both you and Archie Bowlan?"

"I have to admit, it did give them a problem. But I talked them into leaving it up to the good people of Deadwood.

So they've decided to have a vote. The winner gives them the water."

Tuck's mind moved back to the meeting he'd attended with Archie and his gang. "So that means if you win the right to give Deadwood the water, Bowlan will have to find another use for his water or he'll have to give it up."

"Exactly," said George as he let fly a blob of tobacco juice. "But first, I've got to be sure they can't make that pollution charge stick." As was his usual habit, he got up, clasped his hands behind his back and started pacing back and forth.

When George was passing, Tuck asked, "You think you can win in court?"

"It might be tough. Now if I remember right, you said Pat Flavin had you round up a couple down and out miners so he could locate them on some abandoned claims downstream from Deadwood."

Tuck nodded and said, "And he's going to pay them to testify against the Homestake."

George went back to his pacing. After a minute or so, he stopped and looked as if he was going to say something then changed his mind. With his hands still clasped behind his back he resumed pacing. What was going through the old man's head? And what part was Tuck going to play?

Finally George stopped, looked down at Tuck, and said, "Now when you get back into town, here's what I want you to do."

The morning of the day of what people were calling the Great Water Fight broke bright and cool. Tuck got up early and strolled down Main Street looking for signs of trouble. Was there anything else he could have done to help George? Try as he might, he couldn't think of a single thing. Only time would tell if the Homestake could claim victory over Archie Bowlan and the DeSmet. It was amazing how the mere offer of free water to the city of Deadwood had created so much tension and activity.

At first the city officials couldn't agree on who was eligible to vote, but after hours of discussion they decided that anyone claiming Deadwood as his official residence was qualified; no proof would be required and the ballots kept secret. Both the Homestake and DeSmet people had spent loads of money and manpower turning the vote into a popularity contest. Tuck figured their gestures of good will were about as genuine as Charley Utter's giving Kelly her chance to become an actress.

For the past week Tuck had been staying in a hotel in Deadwood. It was Pat Flavin's idea. Flavin wanted him to see if he could get a line on what Hearst had up his sleeve. Tuck grinned, wondering how Flavin was going to react when he found out who Tuck really worked for. Still grinning, he picked up copies of the three local papers and headed back to his room. He was anxious to get an idea of what the opinion writers were saying about the water fight.

When he started reading the *Press*, a knot formed in his stomach. The editorial writer, a man named Snider, was endorsing the DeSmet offer. He claimed the Homestake people were not to be trusted.

Tuck threw down the paper, rolled and lighted a cigarette, then picked up the *Times*. It wasn't as bad. Obviously the editor had made the decision to remain neutral. So far the DeSmet had gotten the better coverage.

He took a long puff and sniffed out the butt before opening up the *Deadwood Pioneer*. The more Tuck read, the better he felt. The Homestake had found a friend. This editor pointed out the superior advantage the Homestake had over the DeSmet for furnishing the city with a full and everlasting supply of pure water. He even went on to say that if the people voted in favor of the DeSmet, they would regret their mistake to the last day of their lives. Tuck was elated. He was beaming with self-confidence as he went back out to look around.

The first thing he did was make the rounds of the six polling places. At each voting booth, he gave a different name and was allowed to vote. And he was not alone. At each place he watched Johnnie Flaherty and his corps of Homestake workers doing the same.

When Johnnie and his crew weren't voting, they were handing out free glasses of champagne at one of the many information booths furnished by the Homestake. Tuck had heard about rigged election, but he'd never witnessed such a flagrant attempt to influence a vote.

Shortly after twelve noon, Tuck passed Hearst on the street and George gave him the sign to put their plan into action.

Tuck nodded to George and went straight to O'Neal's saloon where he'd told Pat and Archie to meet him. At the same time he spotted them at a table in the corner, Flavin stood up and yelled, "Tuck, we're over here."

Tuck sat down, ordered a beer, studied the anxious faces on the two men, and said, "Congratulations, Mr. Bowlan. "I've been to every polling place and I'd bet my shirt you've already got more than enough votes. I don't think we should try to stop any more people from voting."

Both men's faces broke out in smiles. "Wow-e-e-e." Pat yelled in the form of a war whoop.

Archie motioned to one of his foremen. When the husky miner stepped forward, Archie got up and said in a low voice, "Get your men together. Go out there and do whatever is necessary to block the voting booths. But make sure you don't cause any trouble." Archie thought for a second and then said, "Just keep buying everyone drinks. I don't think many of them will pass up a free drink just to vote on free water."

As the miners were going out the door, Pat said, "Tuck, you go and make sure they do their jobs."

Tuck finished his beer, went out and walked around for awhile. When he figured sufficient time had passed, he went back to O'Neal's and reported that all was going well.

Without even bothering to sit down, he left them saying, "I'll be back when the polls close."

Shortly after dark, Tuck, Archie Bowlan, and Pat Flavin waited at O'Neal's saloon for the votes to be counted. Tuck had to hold back a smile when Pat and Archie started bragging about how this election was going to take the wind out of old Hearst's sails.

Pat then ordered another round of beer and six hard-boiled eggs. Being in no mood to watch the disgusting way Pat ate eggs, Tuck shifted his chair and interest to a bunch of miners huddled around the piano, all out of key, trying to sing along with the piano player.

Suddenly the music stopped, the mayor walked out on the stage, and said, "Well folks, the votes have been counted and . . ." Tuck held his breath. "The Homestake has won the right to supply water to Deadwood."

Archie Bowlan leaped to his feet and at the top of his voice yelled, "That can't be right! No way they could've won unless old man Hearst bought off the people tallying the vote."

Then from somewhere across the room, someone yelled, "Instead of cussing old man Hearst, you should be honoring him. It's his money that's goin' to keep the mines going." Tuck had all he could do to keep from laughing.

Pat Flavin grabbed Archie's arm and said, "Settle down, Archie. We've still got the pollution charge—with the witnesses we've got lined up, we're sure to win."

Chapter Seventeen

Tuck gazed out the window at the snow piled deep against the buildings. He pressed his nose to the cold glass and peered up and down the street. It didn't know what he was looking for but whatever it was, wasn't there. Everything standing still was buried in snow and there wasn't a moving soul in sight. He'd heard winters were rough in the Black Hills but never dreamed they'd be this bad.

The snow had started three days ago. That afternoon it had been quite warm and had commenced as rain, but after about an hour it had turned to snow and hadn't let up since. Already in some places it was six or seven feet deep. In drifts it was even higher. So this was what they call cabin fever? There was nothing to do except hole up and wait it out.

Not only was cabin fever annoying, but the pollution trial had been delayed, which meant he had no idea when he would be returning to San Francisco. With Kelly performing in so many shows, he didn't get the chance to see her very often, causing time to drag even more. She was always on his mind and the only way to get her out of there was to go back home. He figured the reason the trial was postponed was the judge was afraid of being snowed in with George Hearst and Archie Bowlan. Tuck thought it over and decided it wasn't such a bad idea. The delay could cause a real problem though if the witnesses he'd spent over two weeks lining up somehow disappeared. Time was standing still and this double life had gone on far too long. He had to get that blasted trial behind him.

Tuck put a fresh stick of wood in the little stove before he pulled over a chair next to it and started reading *Roughing it*. George had loaned him the book, but only after spending several minutes telling him what good friends he and Mark Twain were. Of course he had called him Sammy Clemens. Tuck wasn't too impressed with the book itself because the story wandered too much. Although, he did think Clemens was clever and it was interesting how the lives of the forty-niners were so different from the miners in the Black Hills. If Clemens had stuck to the gold rush, it would be better reading. Just as Tuck started turning a page, a sudden knock on the door froze him in place for a second. He put down the book and went to see who it was.

He was shocked to see Kelly standing there shivering, her clothes covered with snow. The perplexed expression on her face told him something was wrong. She stamped her feet and shook her arms, but snow still stuck to her green cape. Tuck grabbed her arm and dragged her through the door. "What on earth are you doing out on a day like this? Take that cape off and stand by the fire. I'll pour you a brandy to take the chill off."

As he poured the brandy he wondered what problems she was bringing him this time. Seemed as if every time she showed up unexpectedly, he found himself involved in something that was really none of his business. But so what. He was still glad to see her and she was even more beautiful than he'd remembered.

Kelly took a sip of brandy and said, "Tuck. If you only

knew how much I hate to bother her, but I'm worried and you're the only one I can turn to."

The anxiety in her eyes tempted him to take her in his arms. But instead, he asked, "What's got you so worried?"

She gripped his hand. "You're probably going to think I'm crazy, but I had a horrible dream last night. A dream so real I can't get it out of my mind."

Tuck took his hand from her grasp and used both hands to lightly squeeze her shoulders. "Come on now, Kelly," he said gently. "A dream is just a dream and it can't be that bad. Tell me about it. Maybe I can make you feel better."

"Ira's in trouble, Tuck. The only way I can feel better is if we go and see him."

Her words left Tuck without anything else to say except, "What kind of trouble?"

"I'm not sure," she said. "I just know he needs help."

Tuck frowned.

She pulled away and said, "See, I knew you wouldn't believe me."

He moved closer. "It's not that I don't believe you. I just don't believe in dreams coming true."

"But this different," she pleaded. "Armstrong kept barking. Like he was trying to tell me something. Because Ira wasn't there, I'm sure Armstrong was telling me he needed help." She reached for her cape. "If you won't go with me, I'll go alone. I'm sure if I don't, Ira is going to die."

He took her shoulders again and stared into her deep blue eyes. "Please settle down. If it'll make you feel better, I'll hike out there and check on him." He thought of the difficult task of fighting the deep snow, and said, "But I'm going alone."

Tuck stood on the edge of the cliff overlooking the canyon. It was already mid-afternoon. Normally the trip took four hours. But now he'd been on the trail for six and still had a ways to go. The first hour had been the slowest. It seemed as if he was never going to get the hang of walking on the teardrop shaped snowshoes. When he finally got used to them, he made pretty good progress, but it was tiring work and took a lot of strength and energy. Still they were better than plowing through the deep drifts.

The canyon floor below was covered in a heavy blanket of white. Only the tops of some leafless trees broke the surface. Even the beaver dams were invisible. On the far side of the canyon, the tall evergreens looked black against the snow. Nothing moved. The only sound came from the squeaking snow beneath his feet. Even the birds and wild-life had more sense than he did. They were holed up in their hiding places and not venturing out in this weather. But something was bothering him. What was it? What was missing?

Suddenly Tuck realized what it was. There was no smoke. He should be able to see smoke from the cabin rising through the tall evergreens. A knot formed in his stomach. Maybe Kelly was right. There is no reason why Ira wouldn't have a fire going.

Of course it's possible that Ira isn't at the cabin. Maybe he'd gone somewhere and hadn't gotten back. But his roll-ing gut told him he was only fooling himself. He was sure there was something wrong. If there was a chance to save Ira, Tuck had to hurry.

He quickly started down the steep incline. He'd only taken a half dozen steps when his snowshoes became en-tangled, causing him to lose his balance and pitch forward. Head over heels he tumbled down the slope, spending more time in the air than on the snow. When he finally came to rest, he was on the canyon floor looking up at the trail he'd made on the way down. It looked like the tracks of a huge animal. Did he break anything? Would it be safe to move? But then he remembered Ira and that he had to get up and find him.

Tuck struggled to get the snowshoes under him. After several unsuccessful attempts, he dragged himself to a tree and pulled himself upright. He took a few steps to test for broken bones. Nothing seemed unusual. He'd be sore in the morning, but for now he had to get to Ira.

When he broke out of the forest and into the clearing he stared at the cabin and his heart jumped to his throat. Snow was piled high against the door. No one had been in or out. Ira was either dead or not at home. He prayed for the latter. Then he heard mournful baying coming from inside. He pictured the worst for his old friend.

At first he tried clearing the snow with his hands. It was too slow. He took off one of his snowshoes and started pushing it aside. As he worked, the baying never stopped and there was no sign of Ira. Soon as he worked his way down to the door handle, he pushed open the door and rushed inside. It was as cold inside as out and there was a smell of death hanging in the air.

Armstrong slowly rose up from Ira's bunk, jumped down, and came running to Tuck. He quickly turned, trotted back across the room, and crawled upon the bunk again. A weak cough came from beneath the blankets. "Ira!" Tuck shouted. "Are you all right?" There was no answer and worst of all, no movement.

Tuck leaned across the dog and lifted the blanket and pleaded, "Ira, Ira. It's me, Tuck. Can you hear me?" There was no response.

Tuck placed his shaking hand on Ira's forehead. The old man was burning up, but at least he was still alive. Maybe he'd made it on time and there was still a chance. Tuck quickly replaced the blanket, took off his coat and laid it on top. Then he hurried to the stove, put in some pitch-pine kindling, and started a fire. He did the same in the fireplace.

Only when the room started to warm did Armstrong crawl off Ira's bunk and head for his water bowl. It was frozen solid. Tuck put the bowl and water-bucket on the stove to melt.

When it seemed he'd done all he could do at the time,

Tuck took a deep breath and sat down at the table to try to figure out what to do next. When Armstrong came to his side, Tuck bent down, patted the dog's head, and said, "You knew you were keeping Ira from freezing, didn't you? I don't know what we're going to do, but we're not going to let him die." Armstrong brought forth a low whine giving Tuck the feeling the dog understood everything he had said. Tuck kneeled down and hugged the large wolflike dog. "First thing we must do is get some nourishment in him. I'll bet you're hungry too."

Tuck stood up and took down a haunch of smoked venison hanging above the work counter. He cut off several strips, threw one to Armstrong, and dropped the rest into a pot of water.

Several minutes later, as the pot boiled, the clear water had changed to a rich caramel-colored broth. It smelled good. He tasted it. It was good. He spooned the steaming liquid into a bowl, took it to Ira, and kneeled at his side. He used his left hand to raise the semiconscious old man to a sitting position. Feeding Ira was hard and slow going. After several minutes he'd only managed to get a few spoonfuls down. Tuck became worried and said, "Ira, we've got to get the rest of this broth into you or I'm afraid you won't be strong enough to make the trip back to Lead. We must get you to a doctor."

Then Ira's eyelids twitched twice, and then opened a crack. His lips, almost hidden by the salt and pepper stubble, whispered, "Spearfish. It's easier." A sudden cough ended his words.

Tuck felt a surge of relief as he said, "Ira! Thank goodness you're awake. First thing tomorrow morning I'm getting you and Armstrong out of here."

Ira stopped coughing long enough to say, "Take me to Spearfish. It's all downhill."

Tuck gave Ira another spoonful as he said, "My friend, if you want to go to Spearfish, that's where we'll go. I just hope there's a doctor there."

"There is." Ira weakly pushed the spoon away. He closed his eyes. His body went limp, his head fell back. Tuck's heart pounded as he reached for a pulse. He found it. It was weak, but it was there. Ira was only sleeping.

While the old man slept, Tuck paced the floor trying to figure out how he was going to get Ira to Spearfish. Finally, tired of pacing, he dropped onto the bent-willow settee and rested his left hand on the curved arm. Curved, he thought, like a sled runner. Tuck jumped up and grabbed his coat, his mind going a mile a minute.

He went out and around the corner to get the bucksaw. The deep snow made it rough going. By the time he'd reached the woodpile, he realized his first plan wouldn't work. The thin arms on the settee would just dig in; he'd end up pulling dead weight. What he needed was something with a wide smooth surface. But then he leaned against the cabin wall and felt the bearskin Ira had nailed up to dry. It was stiff as a board as he pulled it loose, grabbed the bucksaw, and went inside. It just might be what he needed.

After spreading the huge skin on the floor, fur side up, Tuck took the bucksaw and cut the settee into pieces. Then he reassembled the pieces into the shape of a toboggan and bound them together with rawhide strings. Satisfied with its shape and strength, Tuck slid the frame into the center of the open bearskin.

Tuck stepped back, admiring his handiwork. The thing should work. In the morning he'd put a mattress on the frame, lay Ira on the mattress, and pile blankets on top. Then he'd wrap the bearskin around both the frame and Ira. He felt he'd accomplished something. By this time tomorrow, he'd have Ira down the canyon and in the hands of a doctor. But now he needed some rest himself.

An hour before dawn, Tuck rolled out and built up the fire. During the night, he got up three times to check on Ira. Each time he managed to get a few more spoonfuls of broth into him. The trip down the canyon was going to be rough on the frail old man. The more nourishment he could get down him, the better his chances.

By first light they were ready. Ira was awake, but weak. Amazed by how light the old man was, Tuck lifted him from his bunk and laid him on the sled. He then took Ira's hot-water bottle and filled it with the remainder of the hot broth, which he placed, along with a tin cup and small candle, next to Ira. "We'll need these on the trail," said Tuck. Ira didn't answer.

For the final step, Tuck folded a flap of the furry bearskin over the lower half of Ira's body, moved around to his head and drew the hide up over the curved front of the frame. He then checked to make sure Ira would get plenty of fresh air. Satisfied, he folded over the two side flaps. Ira was as snug as a moth in a cocoon.

After putting out the fires, Tuck pulled the sled out into the snow saying, "Come on, Armstrong, we've got to get our friend to a doctor."

The makeshift sled glided easily over the snow. Sometimes too easily. Whenever the trail dipped sharply, it ran up onto the back of Tuck's snowshoes. But by the end of the first hour he'd learned what to expect and guided it alongside him.

Armstrong was the one having trouble. He kept breaking through the soft snow and couldn't keep up. Finally, Tuck picked him up and put him on the sled with Ira. The added weight made his job a bit harder, but they were still making good time.

Halfway down the canyon, Tuck heard the roar. He looked up. It was coming from somewhere above him. The glare of bright sun on the white snow prevented him from seeing what was making the noise. But then huge pine trees started falling and he knew what it was. The whole mountain was sliding in their direction.

Sweat formed on his brow. His gut churned. What could he do? There was no escape. He'd never be able to outrun it. Then he looked around and spotted a slight hollow in the canyon wall.

Tuck quickly dragged the sled and shoved it into the shallow opening. He then braced himself by spreading his legs and placing his hands against the cold wall hoping his body would shelter Ira from the cascading snow and rocks. His knees were shaking. He'd never be able to hold off the weight, but he had to try.

The roar grew. First, thundering, then pounding, and then a loud crash. Suddenly they were in total darkness. Tuck felt a weight on his back, but it didn't feel like snow. Twisting his head, he got a face full of needles. He wasn't sure, but he guessed that a tall pine tree was leaning against the canyon wall protecting them. The roar continued. The snow slide went on. But they weren't being crushed.

Finally the roar stopped. It was pitch dark. He prayed that the tree would hold. Tuck knelt down, reached under the bearskin and took out the candle. He struck a match and lit the wick. Ira was awake, but oblivious to what was going on. Probably that was good. It was a miracle they were still alive. But now how was he going to get them out of there?

He kicked off his snowshoes and used one of them to try and poke a hole through the piled up snow. It was no use. He had to come up with another plan. He wasn't about to give up without a fight. While he was thinking, he'd heat up some of the broth for Ira. After several spoonfuls, the old man had had enough. He lay there staring into space. Watching the old man gave Tuck a funny feeling. The candlelight was dim, but he'd swear Ira was staring up at something and trying to give him a message.

Tuck eased himself around and put his back against the canyon wall. There it was. It must be what Ira was looking at. Several feet above them, tiny slivers of bright sunlight showed through the thick branches. If he could climb up there, he'd be above the snow line.

Bracing his back against the wall and using the tree

branches to pull himself up, he was able to lean forward and stick his head out into the bright sunlight. He'd done it. But now, how was he going to free Ira and Armstrong? It took him almost an hour to go back down and, using Armstrong's long leather leash, pull Ira and the sled to freedom. He then went back for Armstrong.

Within minutes they were on their way. The canyon was strewn with downed trees, huge stones, and giant piles of gravel-filled snow. It was taking longer, but at least they were moving again.

As the canyon grew wider and the land grew flatter, Tuck saw smoke rising in the distance. It had to be Spearfish. They had made it but his job wouldn't be finished till he got Ira to a doctor. In another hour and a half, that was done. The doctor took Ira into his own house and started treating him. He wasn't sure what it was, but from the sound of his lungs he figured it was pneumonia. He also said it would take some time before he was ready to go back home.

Soon as he was satisfied Ira was being taken care of, Tuck went to the telegraph office and sent a message to George telling him to pass it on to Kelly.

Chapter Eighteen

After a month of bad weather, the day of the water pollution trial finally arrived. Tuck sat in the back row of the courtroom. Although deep drifts of snow still lined the streets and roads, people were able to move around and live a near normal life again.

Ira was still recovering from his bout with pneumonia. It had been touch and go for a few days, but the doctor wouldn't give up. Gradually he got stronger and was about ready to go home. Soon as the trial was over, Tuck planned to rent a sleigh so he and Kelly could go down to Spearfish, pick Ira up, and take him back to his cabin.

Tuck was so proud of Kelly. She'd already played several roles and played them well. There was no longer any doubt that she was really a good actress with a great future. A future that had no room for a never-at-home detective. She'd even stopped flying off the handle, which greatly improved her chances of not getting into any more trouble. That fact alone took a heavy load off his mind. Now he and George could go back to California without worrying about her. He sighed. He was going to miss her and Ira. But they had their lives to live and he had his.

The courtroom was filling up. Kelly, Mr. and Mrs. Langrishe, and two men Tuck recognized as actors came in and took seats across the aisle. None of them showed any sign of their knowing him. He turned around and looked at the door just as George came in stomping the snow off his feet. He was followed by the Homestake attorneys. The three of them, stiff necked and looking straight ahead, marched to the front and took seats at a table to the left of the judge's bench. A minute or so later, Archie Bowlan and Pat Flavin waddled in and occupied the table to the right.

Judge Moody, in his long black robe, entered through a door behind the bench. He quickly banged his gavel and called the court to order. Tuck smiled. It was the beginning of the end. By the time this trial was over he'd be through with Pat Flavin and Archie Bowlan, and, in a few days, be on his way back to California. What a relief it would be not to worry about anyone but himself again. He was hoping George would give him a good recommendation. Maybe Chief Hume would assign him to the hunt to bring in Black Bart.

Judge Moody spoke, "What we have today is a civil complaint brought by Mr. Bowlan and the DeSmet Mining Company against the Homestake Mining Company. Mr. Bowlan charges the Homestake with polluting the water in Boulder Ditch and Whitewood Creek." He stared at Archie Bowlan and asked, "Is that correct?"

Pat Flavin stood up and said, "That is correct, your honor."

"I take it you are representing, Mr. Bowlan," said the judge.

"That's also correct, your honor."

Judge Moody turned to the Homestake table. "The Homestake will be represented by you, Mr. Thomas?"

Thomas rose partway. "Correct again, your honor."

"Very well. Mr. Flavin, do you have an opening statement?"

Pat hauled his huge body from his chair, dawdled before the bench, and looked up at Judge Moody. "I do, your honor." He turned toward the Homestake table and pointed. "We intend to show that George Hearst and his mining company are causing irreparable damage to the water supply of this whole area." He paused for a second and shook his head. "Your honor, this is not just a matter of concern for the people of Lead and Deadwood, but for everyone whose property touches the miles and miles of stream and riverbanks below."

Pat shook his finger at George. "That man there and his partners back in San Francisco don't care what they are doing to our water. They milk the earth for its gold and when they get all they can grab, they move on. The rest of us are left with the devastation of their greed."

Judge Moody held up his right hand. "We don't need any long winded speeches. You'll have a chance to prove your charges, but it'll have to be done with more than rhetoric." He looked at the Homestake table and asked, "Mr. Thomas, do you have an opening statement?"

Thomas rose to his feet, and said, "We do not, your honor."

"Very well then. Mr. Flavin, call your first witness."

"Thanks, Judge. My first witness will be Pete McDougal."

A skinny little man wearing an oversized Union Army overcoat and rubber boots got up, shuffled forward, and took the stand.

When Pat positioned his huge body in front of the little man, Tuck had trouble seeing the witness. But when Pat started asking questions, Tuck heard him loud and clear.

"Mr. McDougal. Please tell the court what you do for a living."

Tuck grinned as the little man said, "Shucks, Pat. Ya

know what I do for a living. You and that guy sitting back there"—he pointed at Tuck—"are the ones what hired me."

Pat, obviously aggravated, said, "Mr. McDougal, it doesn't matter what I know. Tell the judge what you do for a living."

The little man shrugged. "Take a strain, Pat. No use getting all bent out of shape." He turned to the judge and said, "I got me a job washin' gold out of an old mining claim on Split Tail Hill."

Pat rubbed his hands together. "That's better. Now tell the judge where you get the water you need to wash the gold."

"I get it from the only place I can. Boulder Ditch."

"Now, Pete. Will you tell us if the water is clean?"

McDougal pondered for a second. "Well, I wouldn't want to drink it."

Pat stared at the witness, then said in a loud voice, "Mr. McDougal, isn't it a fact that the water you use to wash your sluice-box is so dirty you can't separate the gold from the gravel—"

Thomas jumped up. "I object, your honor. Mr. Flavin is putting words in the witness's mouth."

"Objection sustained. Mr. Flavin, you can ask the questions, but you must let the witness provide the answers."

Pat gave Thomas a dirty look. "Mr. McDougal, tell the judge about the problems you're having with the water."

McDougal shrugged again and said, "Judge. I'm havin' problems just like Pat said."

Judge Moody shook his head. "You got anything else to say?"

McDougal looked at Pat and said, "Did I say all you wanted me to?"

Pat Flavin didn't answer. "No further questions, your honor."

Under cross-examination, McDougal admitted that Archie Bowlan owned the claim on Split Tail Creek, and that he hadn't found even a trace of gold on it.

Pat's next witness was John Andrews, owner of a Deadwood laundry. After the preliminaries, Pat asked, "Mr. Andrews, do you have a contract to purchase water from Boulder Ditch?"

"I do."

Pat strolled from the witness stand to this table and back again. "Mr. Andrews, do you use the water from Boulder Ditch?"

"No, I don't."

Pat was once again rubbing his hands and smiling. "Why don't you use the water from Boulder Ditch?"

"Because the clothes won't come clean."

"Why?"

"The water contains every mineral known to man."

Pat looked like he had the world by the tail. "And where do all those minerals come from?"

John Andrews, sounding well rehearsed, said, "Well. I would say they come from the mines upstream."

"Do you know the names of the mines?"

"The only one I know, is the Homestake."

Pat smirked at George, turned to Judge Moody, and said, "No further questions, your honor."

Under cross-examination, Mr. Thomas asked, "Mr. Andrews, where do you now get the water for your laundry?"

"I get it from City Creek."

"Is the water clean?"

"Of course or I wouldn't use it."

Now it was Thomas looking confident. "Mr. Andrews, do you have a contract to provide laundry services to the DeSmet Mining Company?"

Andrews looked surprised. He glanced at Archie Bowlan.

Judge Moody said, "Answer the question."

Looking uncomfortable, Andrews said, "Yes, I do."

Thomas was like a leopard ready to strike. "Mr. Andrews, is it not true that if you didn't sign that contract to purchase water from Boulder Ditch the DeSmet Company would have canceled their contract?"

As Andrew hesitated, Tuck wondered how he was going to get around that question. Finally he said, "Well . . ."

Thomas stopped him and said, "Please answer yes or no."

Andrew's blushed. "I guess you could say that would happen."

"They would cancel your contract?"

"Yes."

"No further questions," said Thomas.

On re-direct, Pat tried his best to get the witness to say that City Creek couldn't supply the amount of water he needed, but the damage had already been done.

When it was the Homestake's turn to call witnesses, Tuck started getting nervous. Up till now he was sure they would call him as a witness and he was looking forward to getting this whole double life thing over with. Now he just hoped he could sound credible as he blew the whistle on Bowlan and Flavin. He pictured the looks on their faces when they realized whom Tuck was really working for. Boy, old Pat would probably eat three dozen eggs trying to get his gut to settle down.

Judge Moody looked down at the Homestake table and said, "Mr. Thomas, does the defendant wish to call witnesses?"

Thomas rose slowly to his feet and said, "We have several, your honor." He grinned as he gave Pat Flavin a glance. "As our first witness, we call Mr. Tucker C. Powells."

When Tuck started toward the witness stand, Flavin turned and scowled at him. Tuck returned the scowl with a big smile. Then Pat leaned close to Archie, his mouth going like a chattering squirrel. All of a sudden he stopped, jumped up, faced the judge, and said, "Your honor, may I approach the bench?"

Judge Moody glanced at Thomas, then back to Pat. "You may approach the bench."

Tuck strained to hear what was being said. They were too far away; he couldn't catch a word. Then they stopped talking and Judge Moody asked Mr. Thomas to join them.

Something was going on, but what? Judge Moody picked up his gavel, gave three quick taps, and said, "The court will be in recess for a few minutes. Mr. Hearst, would you and Mr. Bowlan join me and your attorneys in my chambers?"

Tuck stood in the aisle not knowing what to do. Should he take the witness chair or should he go back to his seat? He decided to do neither and instead took a seat next to Kelly and the Langrishes.

They wanted to know what was going on, but he had to tell them that he didn't know any more than they did. Kelly started talking about Ira and how she was looking forward to the trip to bring him home. Tuck found it hard to carry on a conversation. He kept thinking about what was going on back there in Judge Moody's chambers.

Twenty minutes later, Archie and Pat came out followed by George and his attorney, Thomas. Bringing up the rear was Judge Moody.

The judge tapped his gavel again and sat down. Tuck moved toward the witness stand. Judge Moody looked at him and said, "You can go back to your seat, Mr. Powells. Your testimony won't be necessary." He waited till Tuck was back in his seat, then said, "It pleases the court to announce that both parties have agreed to settle this matter. But first, the court finds no basis for the complaint brought against the Homestake." Judge Moody paused for a second. "And second, the court declares that the DeSmet Mining Company has not satisfactorily demonstrated it has a valid use for the water in Boulder Ditch."

A roar went up. Tuck heard Kelly yell, "Yea Judge." Moody pounded his gavel and shouted, "This court will come to order." The crowd settled down. "I will not tolerate any more outbreaks. Now we will get back to business. Both parties have agreed to the following resolution: The

Homestake will return control of Boulder Ditch to its original owners. The DeSmet will give control of Boulder Ditch to the Homestake. In return, the Homestake will pay the DeSmet a sum of thirty thousand dollars." He rose to his feet and announced, "This matter is closed." He gave a heavy tap with his gavel, turned, and left the room.

The spectators went wild, but Tuck didn't wait around. He was in no mood to face Pat Flavin or Archie Bowlan. He rushed out and went straight to his room. Later he'd learn from George what transpired behind those closed doors.

Chapter Nineteen

"Ira, when Tuck and I go back to town, are you sure you'll be able to take care of yourself?" Kelly asked as she sat on the edge of Ira's bunk grasping his bony old hand.

Ira gave her fingers a light squeeze and said, "Now honey, don't you worry about old Ira. Me and Armstrong will be just fine."

She leaned over and gave him a kiss on his brow. "Nevertheless, I think I'm going to send Jack Langrishe a message asking him to get someone else to play my part. I'm staying here till I'm sure you're all better."

"No you're not, young lady. Tuck tells me you're a very talented actress, and I don't want to stand in your way. What's that old saying? 'The show must go on.' "

Kelly stared at her old friend. How puny he still looked. She shuddered at how he must have looked when Tuck found him near death in the cabin. "Ira, I can always get another part, but you're the best friend I've got. I'll never find another you."

"Stop now, Kelly. I'm going to be just fine. Tuck is going to fill the woodbox and shovel a path. Other than those two things, I can handle everything else. As you can see, I've got plenty of food." Ira took a deep breath before saying, "Now I don't want to hurt your feelings, but the fact is, it'll be a pleasure for me and Armstrong to be all by ourselves again."

Kelly turned loose of his hand, got up and walked around the room. She returned to his bunk, looked down at him and said, "Tell you what. We'll spend the night and see how you look in the morning. But I'll tell you right now, if I still don't like the way you look, I'm staying here."

With a wry smile, Ira said, "Don't get uppity, girl. If you're so worried about me, why don't you make us some supper? A big batch of hotcakes and bacon would sure taste good."

"All right," she said. "But don't think this is the end of our discussion." She hurried to the kitchen section of the cabin and put on an apron. As she mixed the flour, baking soda, and canned milk, she wondered what she should do. When Tuck finished shoveling the paths to the privy and spring, she'd talk it over with him.

By the time Tuck and Armstrong came back in, a huge plate of bacon stood in the open warming oven. As he hung up his coat, she dipped her fingers in a cup of water, moved her hand over the stovetop, and sprinkled the waiting griddle. The drops danced like popcorn over a hot fire, then disappeared. Kelly glanced at Tuck, smiled, and said, "You're right on time. Why don't you help Ira to the table while I pour the batter?"

Ira raised up in his bunk and said, "Now Tuck, don't you pay her no mind. I can take care of myself. Just hand me one of those sticks." He pointed to what was left of the settee. "I'll get to the table on my own. Might as well get used to taking care of myself."

Out of the corner of her eye she watched Tuck pick up a straight piece of willow and lean on it to make sure it would support Ira's weight. Satisfied, he handed it to Ira, turned back to her, and said, "Sure hope you made plenty of bacon or you and Ira might not get any. I smelled it cooking all the way down to the spring. It smelled so good, I could taste it." He chuckled and poured himself a cup of coffee.

"You watch the way you talk, Mr. Powells, or you may not get any bacon. Now you two get to your seats before these griddle cakes turn to leather." She put the platter of pancakes on the table, turned back to the stove, and using a bright red potholder, picked up the bacon. "You having coffee, Ira?" she asked.

"You better believe it," he said.

As she ate, Kelly kept her eyes glued on the old man. The way he downed three huge griddle cakes, four slices of bacon, a cup of coffee, and then took another griddle cake to sop of the last drops of syrup, she felt a bit more confident that he was on the mend.

As she poured him another cup of coffee, he looked up into her eyes, and said, "Them flapjacks were cooked every bit as good as I could do myself." He paused for a second and stared at Tuck. "This lassie is ready to make someone a real fine wife."

What brought that up? Her stomach twitched waiting for Tuck's reply. When Tuck looked at her and smiled, her heart was beating like a woodpecker on a dead tree. Finally he said, "I think you're right, Ira." He took a sip of coffee. "How 'bout it Kelly, you got your eye on one of Jack Langrishe's young actors?"

Kelly jerked off her apron and threw it on a chair. "No, I don't, and I don't expect to either!" She spun around, went to the door and took down her cape. As she was putting it on, she said, "I'm going for a walk." She rushed out, slamming the door behind her.

She ran as fast as she could away from the cabin. Then she stopped, picked up a stick, and started beating the trunk of a large pine tree. Tears flowed from her eyes as she whacked, whacked, whacked till her arm got so tired it felt like it was ready to fall off. She tossed aside the stick, and leaned against the tree knowing she hadn't accomplished a thing, but she felt better. A few minutes later, she bent down, picked up a fistful of snow, and held it against her eyes. She'd die if they noticed she'd been crying.

When she went back inside the cabin, Tuck was clearing the table and Ira was elbow deep in a pan of sudsy water. Kelly hung up her cape and rushed to his side. "What are you doing, Ira? You dry your hands right now and get back in that bunk! I'll do the dishes." She spun around, faced Tuck, and said, "And I don't need any help from you either."

Like scolded dogs, both men stopped what they were doing, put their tails between their legs and got out of her way. As she finished the dishes, she concentrated on what they were saying to each other.

Ira asked Tuck if there was anything new with George and the Homestake. Tuck thought for a minute and said, "George is flying high. Every time they go to court, they win. Except for the DeSmet, he now owns every claim in the vicinity of the Homestake."

"Is he going after the DeSmet?" Ira asked.

Tuck nodded, "George thinks he can buy out Archie Bowlan, but he's going to wait for Archie to make the first move."

Soon as she finished the dishes and sat down by herself at the table, Ira motioned to her and said, "Kelly honey, why don't you join us over here?"

She really did want to, but was afraid to look Tuck in the eye. "It's been a long day," she said. "I feel very tired. I think I'll just sweep the floor and go to bed." She got up and grabbed the broom from the corner behind the stove.

Ira put the end of his cane between his feet and started to stand up. "Kelly, if you're tired, you go to bed now, I'll finish up."

"Tuck," she scolded. "Don't let him get up. He needs the rest more than I do."

Tuck jumped to his feet. Ira sat down, leaned back in

his chair, and as if nothing had happened, asked, "Is George going to stick around till he gets the DeSmet, or is he going to let Sam McMaster handle it.?"

"Sam will take care of it. We're going back to San Francisco next week. Now that Judge Moody is chief counsel for the Homestake, George is not worried about anything going wrong."

Kelly's heart skipped a beat. Going back? She always knew it might happen someday, but not so soon. How was she going to get by without the only man she'd ever loved and trusted? Of course there was Ira and Jack but they were different. She'd trust them with her life, but Tuck was the only one she loved.

Ira lowered his voice and said, "It sounds like you're going too. I was hoping you'd stay in the Hills."

Kelly froze. "Please, Tuck, say you are not going," she said beneath her breath.

Tuck said, "As a matter of fact, George did offer me a job managing the new pumping station they're building in Hanna. He said it was a real important job and he needed someone he could trust."

Ira tapped the floor with his cane. "Why don't you change your mind and take him up on it? You could live here with me till you build yourself a cabin. I'll make sure you don't go hungry."

"Tell you the truth, I did think about it." Tuck got up and stood in front of the fireplace. "But, I've still got my job with Wells Fargo, and I never gave up my flat in Frisco. Most important of all though, is my wife is buried there."

Kelly felt like going back out and pounding the tree. What was the use? Mary Lou always won. Kelly, with a heavy heart, took off her apron and hung it on a hook. Then, without stopping to say good night, she hurried into her underground bedroom and bolted the door. Fighting back tears, she threw herself on her bunk and wondered why her new wonderful world was coming to an end.

* * *

By the next morning, Kelly felt better. She tried again to convince Ira she should stay, but he wouldn't hear of it. When Tuck mentioned that George would be out the next day, she dropped the subject.

Although they were both being extra nice to her, she had a feeling that all was not well between them. When Tuck asked Ira if he had a good night's sleep, Ira didn't answer. Then when Tuck tried to pour Ira a cup of coffee, Ira pulled his cup away and said he'd get his own coffee. Armstrong must have shared her feelings. He'd go from Tuck to Ira, then back to Tuck, and back to Ira. On each trip he nudged their legs with his nose. Obviously he was trying to tell them something, but what was it?

While Kelly made breakfast, Tuck brought in more firewood. To make sure Ira didn't run out, not only did he fill the woodbin, he started a pile where the settee used to stand. By the time breakfast was ready, a two- or three-weeks' supply of wood was stacked in the middle of the room.

"Time for breakfast, boys," called Kelly.

The two men sat opposite one another. Kelly watched as they downed their ham and eggs without acknowledging each other's presence.

Then, having reached a point where she couldn't stand it anymore, she poured them a cup of coffee, put the pot back on the stove, faced the two men, and with hands on hips, said, "I don't know what's eating you two, but you're both acting like babies. I'm not going back to town till whatever is bothering you gets straightened out. You'd better be talking to one another soon." She lifted her cape from the hook and headed for the door. Before going out, she turned and said, "Good friends shouldn't treat each other the way you two are doing."

She stayed outside for about ten minutes and then went back in. Tuck had slid his chair around and was sitting next to Ira. They looked up at Kelly, guilt written all over their faces.

Tuck got up and reached for his jacket. "I'm going down to the ice cave to bring up some meat. We'll put it in Kelly's room. Once the fire goes out in there, it'll stay good and cold."

He was halfway out the door when Ira yelled, "Better bring me a few bottles of beer while you're at it."

Tuck turned around and came back. "Anything else while I'm down there?"

Ira smiled and said, "Can't think of another thing."

Before leaving the cabin, Tuck glanced at Kelly and said, "Why don't you make a list of the dry goods Ira might need. George can bring them out with him."

Even as the horse was hitched to the sleigh, Kelly still wasn't sure she was doing the right thing. But the old man was set in his ways and nothing she said made a difference. He even insisted on going outside to see them off.

Watching the two men hug one another, Kelly felt she had accomplished something. Then after promising Ira he'd come out once more before leaving for California, Tuck climbed onto the sleigh and used the reins to give the horse's rump a tap. His muscles tensed and the sleigh started gliding down the trail.

For as long as the cabin was in sight, Kelly watched the frail old man leaning on his stick, all the time wondering if she was doing the right thing.

Tuck kept the horse and sleigh to the trail they broke on their way in, but it was still slow going. Time after time she wanted to say something, but was always afraid it wouldn't come out right. She sat there in silence staring at the horse struggling through the heavy snow. Finally she couldn't take it anymore. She turned to Tuck and asked, "Did you ever see so much snow in your life?"

"Can't say I have. From what I hear, it's like this every year. Old Mother Nature plays a tough game of poker in these parts. Takes strong-willed people to survive."

"Then why are you going back to San Francisco?"

Tuck jerked his head in her direction, and asked, "What do you mean by that?"

"I just meant that you're strong-willed. Every time we ran into a problem, you took care of it. Ira would be dead if it wasn't for you, and only heaven knows where I'd be."

Tuck didn't reply.

A couple of minutes later, Kelly asked, "Tuck, do you know what Ira told me?"

"What?"

"He said that Mrs. Hearst is twenty-two years younger than George."

"So."

"Well, you're, you're only ten years older than me."

Tuck shook his head. "I wouldn't call that a marriage. They're never together. He's out here and she's traipsing around Europe with their son."

It wasn't the answer she wanted. She bit her lip and pulled the cape tighter around her.

When they reached Cheyenne Crossing, Tuck gave the horse a snap of the reins that sent him trotting over the hard packed snow covering the heavily traveled road to Lead City.

Tuck seemed to have an answer for everything, Kelly thought. Maybe she'd be better off if she just forgot about the whole thing. After all, if they did get married she'd probably spend the rest of her life living with Mary Lou's ghost.

After twenty minutes without either of them saying a word, Tuck pulled up on the reins, bringing the sleigh to a gentle stop. He turned to her, put his hand on her knee, and said, "Look, Kelly. I know you appreciate me helping you out of a couple of scrapes, but that doesn't mean you owe me anything."

She gazed into his warm blue eyes. Was he joking? Could he be that dumb? Finally she said, "Owe you something? What on earth do you mean by that?"

His expression was dead serious. "Well, you keep hinting

about us getting married. Ira even said that you wanted to and that he thought it was a good idea. I figure the only reason you'd want to is either because you think you owe me something or feel sorry for me. Otherwise why would a beautiful young girl want someone like me?"

She shook her head and through tight lips said, "Owe you something? Feel sorry for you?"

"Yes. Because of Mary Lou."

Kelly felt the blood rush to her face. She stood up and started climbing down from the sleigh. Tuck grabbed her arm and said, "Where're you going?"

She jerked her hand away and threw her head back, causing her hood to slide off. Then with hands on hips, and her feet spread in the milk-white snow, she said in a disgusted voice, "Listen to me, Mr. Tucker C. Powells. First of all, I don't think I owe you anything. And second, I may be sorry you lost your wife, but life has to go on. Nothing you or I can do will bring her back. And you might as well get it through that thick head of yours that she has nothing to do with the way I feel about you!"

He looked stunned, like he'd been scratched by a wildcat.

She reached back, pulled the hood over her rust-colored hair, climbed back on the sleigh, and tapped him on the shoulder. When their eyes met, she said, "Before I shut up, I want you to know that I'm sick and tired of you treating me like a little girl. I'm a woman. If you can't see that, you're not the man I think you are. Now get this thing going so you can drop me off at the hotel." With a crack of the whip, the horse took off in a full run.

A few minutes later, he tried putting his hand on her knee again. She brushed it off and said, "Keep your hands off me. The way I feel now, I don't care if I ever see you again, and I wouldn't marry you if you was the last man on earth."

Tuck stared straight ahead without uttering another sound. Kelly took a deep breath and wished she could take back her words.

Chapter Twenty

Tuck tilted his head to let the water flow from the brim of his Stetson. For the past two days it had been raining steadily, with no hint of a sign of letting up. The rain didn't really bother him. In fact it made it easier to convince himself that getting out of the Black Hills was the right decision. He'd thought about it all night and it was still on his mind when he met George at his hotel this morning so they could walk down to the depot together. Now as they waited for the stage to Cheyenne, he was still having doubts. It was more the thought of leaving Kelly than the Black Hills that was causing his concern. Although the sleigh ride from the cabin seemed to sever their relationship for good, he just couldn't accept it as being final. He wished he could explain how he felt about her, but she was such a complicated person it was near impossible. What he did know was that he wished he had her beside him right now.

George couldn't seem to stand still. He kept pacing back and forth, back and forth, Then he'd stop, shake his arms like a duck coming out of a pond, and then stomp his feet like a mad bull. After several stops to shake and stomp,

George walked to the edge of the platform, let loose a jaw full of tobacco juice, turned to Tuck and said, "You don't look too happy, son. Sure you don't want to change your mind about going?"

Was George reading his mind, Tuck wondered as he said, "No, sir. But I wonder where that stage is? It should've been here ten minutes ago."

Hearst shook and stomped. "It'll be here. With all that snow piled up, and now this rain, I imagine it's pretty tough keeping to a schedule." He went back to pacing.

Tuck thought about that last day at the cabin with Kelly and Ira. He wished he was leaving under different circumstances. He hoped he would have seen her at the depot, but with the bad weather and her being in Central City it was probably too much to ask. The paper said she was playing the lead in *Uncle Tom's Cabin*.

If only she wasn't so bullheaded. But maybe it wasn't her at all. Maybe it was him. Did he really treat her like a child? He hadn't meant to. Anyway, it was too late now. If there was only some way he could start over. For sure he'd never say any thing as stupid as evidently he had.

Truth was, she didn't need him anymore than he needed her. Heaven only knows what that miner would have done if she hadn't coldcocked him with that pick handle. Ira was on her side too. He really got mad that night at the cabin. Called me a jackass for not asking her to marry me. He had thought about it, but what if she refused?

Tuck caught an image in the corner of his eye. George had stopped pacing and was standing next to him. "Maybe the stage has been canceled," Tuck said.

George slipped his right hand under his long beard, shook it, and said, "I doubt it. They'd let us know if it was."

As George went back to pacing, Tuck went back to thinking. Seemed like everyone in Lead City wanted him to marry Kelly. But he liked being on his own and didn't want the responsibility of another wife. The loss of Mary

Lou had devastated him and he didn't think he could stand going through it again.

Suddenly the sound of heavy hoofbeats broke Tuck's thoughts. He looked up Main Street. A lone rider raced toward them. When he pulled up, he yelled at the top of his voice, "Deadwood Creek has turned into a river. Central City and every camp in the gulch are getting washed out. Soon as that wall of water reaches Deadwood, it'll be a goner too."

"Central City!" Tuck turned to George. "Did he say Central City? Kelly's in Central City. I've got to get to her. Would you see that my bag gets back to my room?"

George grabbed his arm. "Wait a minute. How are you going to get there? The roads must be washed out."

Tuck pulled at George's grasp and said, "Let go my arm. I'm going up to Terryville and down the other side. That's the way I first got to Lead City." He broke loose and ran up the hill toward the open cut.

The going was tough. Rain on top of frozen ground and deep snow made the climb almost impossible. As soon as he thought he was making headway, he lost his footing and slid back. Making things worse was sweat mixed with rain running down his forehead and into his eyes.

Why had he treated her like he had? If he had been just a little more understanding she probably would have been at the stage depot to see them off. She would have been safe in Lead City instead of being washed out in Central City.

Everything seemed to be going wrong. It was taking to much time and trouble to get a foothold. He'd never make it over the mountain. Finally he reached the woodpile where he and Kelly had hidden. Sticking through the snow he spotted the handle of an axe.

After another minute of slipping and sliding he had the axe in his hand. It was what he needed. When he'd start sliding, he drove the head of the axe into the ice and pulled himself forward. Time after time he repeated the process.

Twenty minutes later, with sweat pouring and breathing hard, he reached Terryville. Knowing the rest of the way to the top was not nearly as steep, he tossed the axe aside. But after taking two or three steps he realized he might need it again so he went back and picked it up.

As he stood at the top of the ridge looking down into the gulch, he saw that the peaceful little creek he'd crossed on his first day in the hills was now a raging river. Deep water lapped at the hotel porch. But it was still standing. He breathed a little easier when he realized he might make it to Kelly in time. But he had to hurry. If the water kept rising, the hotel would be carried away. The stairway leading up to the porch was already under water.

It was then that he realized that even if he made it down the mountain there was no way to get across the flooded stream. But he had no choice. First he'd go down and then find a way across.

The trip down was faster but just as slippery and dangerous. He sat down on the cold wet ground and used the axe as a brake to control his slide toward the rushing water below. His boots were only inches above the edge when he pulled himself to a stop. Up close the chances of getting across looked even worse. But there must be some way to get across and he must find it. He checked the hotel again hoping to be able to make an estimate of how much time he had. Could it be? Through the pouring rain the cape looked black instead of green, but he knew it was Kelly standing on the porch frantically waving both arms in his direction.

He thought he saw her mouth moving, but the thundering roar of rushing water drowned out her voice. She must have seen him coming down the slope. The sight of her increased his determination to get across. He was a good swimmer, but he knew the current was too strong. Maybe if he could make her understand that she must get to higher ground. After all, the rain couldn't last forever.

Tuck pointed in the direction of the slope behind the

hotel and pushed at the air with his open palm hoping she'd leave the hotel. But she didn't move. She just stood there waving and yelling. He couldn't hear her, but maybe she could hear him.

Making a cone with his hands, he yelled, "Kelly! Get out of there! Go up the mountain!" Still she didn't move. He tried again but it was no use. She obviously couldn't hear him.

Tuck looked down at the water. There was a ridge of water that crossed the flow from one bank to the other. It must be the footbridge. It was completely under water but appeared to be intact. If he held tight to the handrails, maybe he could work his way across.

He checked once more. Kelly was still on the porch and showed no signs of leaving. He had to give the footbridge a try. He put the axe aside and eased himself down into the rushing water.

Compared to the water, the air and rain were warm. In seconds his legs were numb and felt heavy as lead. He held tight to the handrail and leaned into the current. He started making progress. A third of the way across he was beginning to believe he'd make it. He looked up to see what Kelly was doing. She'd left the porch and was standing at the water's edge.

Tuck let go with one hand and tried to motion her back. It was a stupid mistake. He lost his balance; his feet shot out from under him. He grabbed for the rail again but to no avail. The current was too strong. He couldn't get his feet back on the bridge.

Now he lay horizontal in the water. If he let go, he'd be swept down stream. He had to go back. It took all the strength he could master to work hand over hand back to the bank. That was close. He had to find another way. He looked across and saw that Kelly was back on the porch.

Tuck picked up the axe and leaned against it while he fought to catch his breath. Once again he studied the submerged bridge. Two thick ropes running from bank to bank

G. Sam Carr

supported it. Then he had a brainstorm. If he could cut the ropes on this side, the current would sweep this end down stream and across to the other side landing him a few yards below the hotel. It wouldn't be easy; if he couldn't hold on, he'd be a goner. But if it worked, it'd be a fast way to get to Kelly.

The raging water had stretched the ropes tight as fiddle strings. As he held fast with one hand, he worked the cutting edge of the axe back and forth across the first rope. When he had cut halfway through, the current took care of the rest. The second rope went even faster. Soon as the rope parted, Tuck dropped the axe and held on with both hands as the end of the bridge shot downstream, started to swing across, and then stopped in midstream. Raging water surged past him. The bridge was hung up on something under water.

Tuck felt his body growing numb. His hands ached. Then suddenly he felt movement. The bridge was sliding downstream again. But after sliding a couple feet, it hung up again. But then it moved a couple more feet. Obviously it was breaking free, but somehow it didn't feel right. He finally realized that the submerged bridge was heading downstream and not toward the opposite shore. He looked up. Kelly was gone.

He saw that the other end of the bridge was pulling loose. If that happened, he and the whole bridge would be swept away. Should he hang on and hope the bridge would float? If it didn't, he'd be wasting his time and Kelly would be on her own after all.

His end of the bridge moved a few more feet, hung there for a while, and then moved again. With both ends free, it must be working its way around whatever was holding it. Then he realized that somehow he was actually getting nearer to the opposite shore. A little farther and he might make it.

When he tried to spot something to grab onto, he spotted Kelly. In her hands she held a coil of rope. A wave of guilt came over him. After what he'd said to her, she was the one waiting to rescue him.

He'd been in the water for over twenty minutes. Even the numbing caused by the cold wasn't helping the pain in his aching hands and arms. He didn't know how much longer he could hold on. And to make matters worse, the bridge was stuck again. He glanced up at Kelly. She was yelling something. He held his breath trying to make out her words. Over the roar of the rushing water, he faintly heard her say, "Hang on, Tuck! I'll throw you a rope!"

Her mouth kept going a mile a minute but he couldn't make out another word. He wondered if she'd know how to throw the rope to get maximum distance. Maybe she did. In her right hand she held a big loop. The rest of the rope was coiled in her left. With the loop hand she quickly crossed herself, swung the loop around her head, and let it fly. Tuck grabbed for it. But it was a bit too short and he missed it. Within a split second it was washed downstream.

Kelly quickly retrieved the rope and tried again. The same thing happened, but she wouldn't give up. This time, she moved a few feet upstream and closer to the bank. Too close. Tuck saw what was happening and yelled, but it was too late. The bank gave way, plunging Kelly into the churning water. As she was being swept past him, he let go of the bridge and swam toward her.

The fright in her eyes gave him a new surge of energy as she struggled to stay afloat. He swam faster, but the icy water had taken its toil. Even though his mind was ready, his body couldn't live up to its expectations. He took a deep breath and worked harder. Slowly he made progress. Several yards downstream; he caught up with her and pulled her to him. They held tight to one another as the churning water carried them downstream toward Deadwood.

But something else was wrong. Little as Kelly was, she was dragging them both under. "Kelly," he yelled, "it's your cape. It's waterlogged and too heavy. You've got to get rid of it."

She started to say something, but changed her mind and nodded. As he held tight to her left hand, she slipped her right arm out of its opening. That was a mistake. With only one arm holding the spread-out cape, the surging water had a much larger surface to work with. Before he could say another word, the overpowering current pulled her out of his grasp.

"Kelly! Let it go!" he yelled as he swam toward her without gaining an inch. He yelled again. This time she let go of the cape and tried swimming upstream toward him. But it was no use. The current was too strong and she was too small.

Using every bit of strength he could muster, he swam faster. He managed to gain a little, but she was still far ahead. If she didn't make it, he'd never forgive himself for letting her break free. He should have known what was going to happen.

Then he saw it. Sticking out of the water downstream was a large object. He saw wheels. It was an overturned wagon bed. "Kelly, grab hold!" He didn't know if she heard him or not, but as the current swept her past, she locked her arm around one of the spokes. In a second he was alongside her.

They were both out of breath and weak as a newborn. "Kelly," he said. "We've got to rest. We'll stay here for a few minutes and then figure out what we'll do next."

"Tuck," she said excitedly. "It's stopped raining, the sun is breaking through."

He looked at her. Her long red hair hung along the sides of her perfectly shaped head in lumpy strings. One strand was pasted across her tiny little nose. But, at this moment she never looked more beautiful. "Don't worry," he said. "We're going to make it."

She smiled. The sun and the reflection from the water made her eyes a vivid green. "Never crossed my mind we wouldn't," she said. Her words set the both of them to laughing.

A few minutes later, two men appeared on the bank. One threw a rope that landed across the wagon bed. Tuck grabbed it and tied it fast to the wagon wheel. It was all they needed. With Kelly holding tight to his neck, Tuck worked hand over hand to the water's edge. One of the men reached down and helped Kelly out. Tuck was right behind. With water streaming from their faces and their clothes sticking to their bodies, Tuck took Kelly's hands in his. They both stood staring into each other's eyes. Finally Tuck said, "We sure make some pair, don't we?"

Her smile disappeared. "We could," she said, "if you'd give us a chance." She pulled her hands loose and turned her back to him.

Tuck quickly moved around in front of her, pulled her into his arms, and said, "What say we head for Lead City and see if George still has that job open? Then, if you're sure you want an old man like me for a husband, we'll find a preacher."

Kelly leaned back and while still holding tight to him, said, "You're not an old man. And now that I've thought about it, I just might marry you. But only if Ira gives me away and the preacher turns out to be a priest."

Tuck grinned. He was sure he'd found the right woman. Unlike Mary Lou, Kelly would always have the final say.